THE PLAN

by David Steenhoek

BONNEVILLE BOOKS™

Springville, Utah

ISBN: 1-55517-642-9
e.1

Published by Bonneville Books
Imprint of Cedar Fort Inc.
www.cedarfort.com

Distributed by:

Typeset by Kristin Nelson
Cover design by Nicole Cunningham
Cover design © 2003 by Lyle Mortimer

Printed in the United States of America
10 9 8 7 6 5 4 3 2 1

Printed on acid-free paper

Library of Congress Cataloging-in-Publication Data

Steenhoek, David, 1974-
The plan / by David Steenhoek.
    p. cm.
ISBN 1-55517-642-9 (acid-free paper)
1. Life change events--Fiction. 2. Young men--Fiction. I. Title.

PS3619.T4758 P58 2003
813'.6--dc21

                    2002153092

THE PLAN

Dedicated
to hopeless romantics
everywhere

CHAPTER 1

John Edwards opened his eyes and started to pull the covers back. "Why do people have to work at all?" he mumbled out loud. He grabbed for the comforter and closed his eyes for some more precious minutes of sleep.

The answer rested on his Ikea desk: credit card bills, car insurance, car payment, cell phone bill, and college loans. Debt sucks. John closed his eyes again, to no avail. He forced himself out of bed by placing one foot on the floor.

"Please tell me it's Saturday." John knew it was Monday.

John looked at himself in the mirror, then removed the crusty sleep stuff from his eyes. *Good Morning John. I'm going to call in sick,* he thought as he squeezed the last drop of tooth-paste onto his brush.

John gave himself plenty of self-reminders during the day, *I'd better go to the store. I'm out of toothpaste.* Realistically, though, he'd forget to go to the store or maybe he'd make it to the store and forget about the toothpaste altogether. It would only cross his mind that night when he tried to brush his teeth again. That's the way it worked with John, and most guys for that matter. Always out of toilet paper, toothpaste, and napkins but one thing John always had a plenty was cereal—from the 'Captain' to 'Lucky' to 'Apple Jacks' to 'Trix.' You name it. John called it breakfast, lunch, and dinner.

John didn't call in sick. Why? He wasn't sure how many sick days he had left.

"Find out how many sick days you have left." John made a note to himself.

His job was an important one. He entered numbers from stacks and stacks of pages into a computer. The stack in front of him was larger than normal.

What a life! *Someone pinch me*, he thought as his fingers pressed down on the keys. His company called him a 'Data Entry Specialist.' John called it 'monkey labor' because you could train a monkey to do his job. To him monkeys weren't that smart. John could never see the world being taken over by monkeys. He thought *Planet of the Apes* was such a fantasy—never could happen. Dolphins on the other hand, now, that's a different story all together. Dolphins have a secret language and have the whole friendship-towards-human angle working. John believed the world leaders should keep their eyes on the dolphins. You just never know.

This was the typical day for John, entering a stack of numbers into his computer and also finding the time to email his friends. John always came up with an odd and absurd topic; today's was, of course, "Which animal species would most likely take over the world and enslave all humans?" John did anything to get through the day and to take away the monotony of his career.

It wasn't always like this; in fact, when John decided to join his current employer he had many suitors and substantial offers. And why not? John was handsome and a recent graduate from BYU in business, graduating with honors. He even had an opportunity to go overseas and work in Europe for an international company. There was only one problem. It didn't fit in his plan.

"The Plan" was developed during the time he was on his mission. Before John's mission, "The Plan" wasn't in effect. He was too busy dating, having fun, being a teenager, and kissing girls.

One night on a P-Day, John decided it was time to become

a man, to put away childish things—paraphrased from the Apostle Paul. John was well versed in the scriptures. Those early, painfully early mornings of Seminary and years of scripture chase were coming in handy. It was there in his small apartment in Curitibia, Brazil, a world away from his own, that he had an epiphany and "The Plan" was born.

First things first, John would go to BYU after his mission and major in business, finish in three and a half years, graduating with honors. Then John would move home to Southern California where he was raised and join a large Fortune 500 company with room for advancement. Next he'd work his way up in the company and become an executive in four years. Then he'd leave the company and start his own endeavor and be the boss. During that time John would meet a beautiful and spiritual woman to spend all time and eternity with, have four or five great kids, own a large house on the beach, financial freedom, and time to spend with the family. There it was in black and white. "The Plan."

John stared ahead at the computer screen. He moved his mouse back and forth. The screen froze. What happened to "The Plan"? John thought he had it all figured out. Some of "The Plan" came true. John graduated from BYU in three and a half years with honors, thanks to maximum credits, long summers in the library, and his eyes focused on "The Plan." John moved back to Southern California and was hired by a large Fortune 500 company.

The company recruiter said those magic words John was dying to hear. "From where you start you'll be able to look right up through the glass ceiling. The future is yours." The words rolled off the recruiter's tongue like he was reading it from cue cards or a teleprompter.

The future is yours. John liked that. And that did it. He was sold, hook, line, and sinker.

And this is where "The Plan" had gone astray. John was sitting at the same desk he started at three years prior. He had been looking up at the same glass ceiling since the first day he was embraced by his employer.

What went wrong? John didn't know.

John shook his mouse and turned it upside down.

"What's wrong with this thing?" Well, it wasn't the mouse. John pressed Alt-Control-Delete, and ESC-F1-F3, and every-thing else he could think of. Nothing. Absolutely nothing. The screen stayed stagnant. John tried a last attempt. The screen flickered.

"Ah ha. I'm smarter than you. You think you can outsmart me. You're a machine." John stopped speaking to the computer and shook his head. *Why are you talking to a computer? What good is that going to do?* Then John thought, *You never know. I need to show the computer that I'm the boss. I call the shots.*

"Man, my brain must be fried." John looked at the computer screen again. He pressed a couple more keys on the keyboard. "Come on!"

What a waste of energy. John stared at the frozen screen. There was absolutely nothing he could do. A smile started to form on the sides of his mouth. He couldn't help it. The smile led to loud, gut-wrenching laughter. It was the kind of laughter in the office where people poke their heads out of their cubi-cles.

If truth is stranger than fiction, then John believed irony was a part of everyday life. This was his life. Frozen. "The Plan" was frozen as well, on hold waiting for a jumpstart. Things had to change.

Help me!!! John was screaming inside.

CHAPTER 2

George Benson's gifted vocals floated through the air and engulfed the crowd gathered in the cultural hall of the Huntington Beach North Stake building in sunny Orange County, California. In the middle of it all was the wedding party and the infamous "wedding line." The "wedding line" was a Mormon tradition whereby the bride and groom are never able to sit down for even a second or grab a bite to eat during the entire reception. So, they usually starve. They don't care—they just want to get to their hotel room.

John fixed his bowtie and walked up to the 'wedding line.' He gave handshakes and hellos to all the people in the line that he didn't know and finally neared the center. A beautiful bride stood in front of him, glowing. She definitely had "the glow." John congratulated her and gave her a big hug. The groom stood by watching it all transpire. John put his hand out for groom. The groom pushed his hand away and gave John a big hug.

"She's a keeper, Pete. Nice work," John whispered in Pete's ear while he slipped two twenties into his hand.

"You know, that's the last time you get to hug her."

"Maybe I should get a another quick one in while you're still happy. Serious, though, man, congratulations. I'm happy for you." John knew Pete was a good man and he deserved her.

Pete was making progress and John knew it. *The last of my single friend's to go,* John thought. He sincerely was going to miss Pete and even though Pete promised to stay tight, he knew deep down that he'd rarely ever see him again. Once you're married you're pretty much dead to your single friends. Weddings are somewhat happy funerals.

George Benson was finishing and John knew he had only a little time to change the CD. So he made his way over to the DJ booth.

DJ gigs were John's form of sanity and fun. This DJ gig was a favor to his friend. John had known Pete for a long time, since they were deacons together in his family ward in Huntington Beach. They even had their Eagle Courts of Honor together. Pete was one of John's best friends.

It was the first time John had seen most of these familiar faces in a long time. It was going to be one of those nights.

The first couple to approach John was the Nelsons. Brother Nelson owned a roofing company and John worked for him one summer when he was sixteen. Brother Nelson was a burley man with a deep voice, Popeye-like forearms, and a farmer's tan. John had always been fond of the Nelsons and they were likewise impressed with his family.

"How are the folks?" Brother Nelson put out his mammoth hand and met John half way.

"Good. they're visiting my sisters in Utah," replied John.

"How many grandkids do they have now?"

"Twenty-two and one in the oven."

John knew the dreaded question was coming. It was inevitable in this setting not to hear it.

And Sister Nelson, the sweet lady that she was, wasn't afraid to ask, "So, when's your wedding?"

"My wedding? Oh, I don't know." John wanted to crawl into a corner and stay there the rest of the night.

And of course Sister Nelson had to re-phrase her thought, "Is there someone special in your life right now, John?"

John looked at her, trying to find a way out of the conversation. He folded, "No. Not right now Sister Nelson."

"Don't worry. She's out there." Sister Nelson patted him on the shoulder.

"It was good seeing you again, John. Say hi to the folks." Brother Nelson thankfully led his wife away from the DJ booth.

"You too. Take care."

It always happened. Sometimes it was phrased differently: Do you have a girlfriend? You have your eye on anyone? Have you met the person that's going to make your life complete? You're a catch, I'm sure she's out there. Keep looking; it happens when you least expect it. I wish I had another daughter. Translation: What's your problem? Why aren't you married? You're a loser! You're a big loser!

John dreaded these run-ins with families from the ward he grew up in. John was always well-liked in the ward. He sang solos in church when he was younger and had widows always telling his mother what a great young man he was. John served as President of deacons, teachers, and 1st Counselor in the Priests' Quorum. If anyone was, John was the apple of the ward's eye.

Now times had changed. John was not the dimple-faced kid with long eyelashes everyone remembered. John just turned twenty-seven. Twenty-seven! In Mormon years that meant he was almost thirty-five or somewhere near there. Most Mormons at twenty-seven have at least two or three kids. John was single, not dating a soul, and now back among the people who saw his great potential when he was young. What happened?!

He was fine with the brunt of the exchanges and perpetual inquisition. Sometimes, though, he wanted to tell people he had decided to become celibate and would never marry at all. But on second thought he realized he'd cause heart attacks; most of the ward members wouldn't catch on that he was only joking.

"John, it will be okay" was the echoed refrain from twenty or thirty more couples like Brother and Sister Nelson.

John was okay. He had no problems at all. He only wished people would stop saying that to him. *Don't feel sorry for me,* he thought. Then John sat there as Enya was climbing up the scales in the background: *Am I sad? Do I look sad? Why do people keep saying that to me? What is wrong with me?*

John had a very active mind. He was always thinking or making conversation in his head. Back when he was a child people said it was healthy for kids to always be analyzing things in their heads. Today people label it "ADD." Whatever it was, John had it and he had it bad. It was a part of who he was. Maybe it was a form of self-psychoanalysis or maybe it was some other psychological term. To keep it simple, John thought a lot.

Finally John came back to his senses. *There's nothing wrong with me. I just haven't found her yet. At least I'm not over thirty. That's when family members start to think you're gay.* John had friends over thirty who had their parents ask that question on occasion.

John always laughed when he tried to picture what it would be like if his father asked him that question. He could picture the scene sitting with his dad, Stephen, a convert to the church, looking him straight in the eyes and asking those questions.

"Son, I love you. I'll accept you any way you are. Is there anything you'd like to tell me?" Stephen would hope it would be painless.

"No, Dad. I don't think so. What's going on?" John would act like he had no clue what his dad was trying to get at.

"You can tell me anything. You can tell me anything at all. Because you know John that we're taught to love the sinner and hate the sin." Stephen would definitely be uncomfortable with that line of questioning.

"What are you talking about?" John would look at Stephen curiously.

Stephen would take a deep breath and clear his throat. "I don't know how to ask this, but your mother and I have been thinking. You're still single. And you're almost thirty-two."

"Well, just come out with it." John had no idea what he was going to say next.

"Are you gay?" Stephen would have to be blunt.

"What?" John would start busting up, laughing hard.

"You know, do you like men instead of women?" Stephen would try again and start to sweat.

John would say, "You've got to be joking. No, Dad. I like women. I love women. I want to find me a woman." John shook his head.

"Thank goodness. I knew I had to say something but I don't know what I would've done if you had said you did like men." Stephen would breathe a sigh of relief.

"That makes two of us." Then John would laugh again.

"Your mother thought I should ask you because, you know—" Stephen would try to explain himself.

"You can stop now," John would cut him off and try to end it.

Stephen would smile, take a deep breath, hug John, and leave the room.

That was the scene John pictured and yes it was humorous but John really didn't want to have to live it. John had at least three years before his parents would even talk about that alternative.

John really did love women. He had dated a good share of women in his time. For some reason at the present he was in a drought and hadn't had a date in three months. There were girls in his office that had approached him to hang out but he'd already dated non-Mormons and none of those relationships

9

panned out. They wanted more from him than he was willing to give. John was a twenty-seven year old virgin and most Non-Mormons girls he had met thought it was a line. John was just waiting for that special someone.

He looked out at his good friend Pete leading his new wife Brandy on the dance floor. Brandy lifted her head up and glanced into his eyes. The magic was there. That's what John wanted more than anything in his life. He wanted to have someone to have and to hold. Maybe it was because of that particular moment but John started to think about the girls from his past.

The group of girls he thought about were named: the "What If's." The "What If's" were the group of girls who always came to mind when John saw someone who had been in his past and now looked happy with a husband.

John thought about Michelle, his semi-girlfriend from High School. They were never officially an item because John didn't really want a girlfriend, but for all intents and purposes Michelle was his girlfriend. Michelle was cute, seventeen, a cheerleader, had her Young Woman's medallion and most importantly had "the glow." John wondered if he could've done something different with Michelle. Maybe he should've made their relationship official and Michelle would've written him on his mission. He would've had someone waiting for him when he came home. In reality, he knew Michelle would've sent him a "Dear John" and then John ironically would've had a rough two or three months trying to overcome the hardship.

No, Michelle really wasn't a *What If* after all. John had heard she was married, living in Southern California some-where and had three kids. *Good for Michelle*, he thought.

John raced through his brain trying to find the real "What If" girl. *Who's the girl from my past that I could see myself with today?* And then the name Charlotte flashed in his mind.

Charlotte Lynn Lee was someone John hadn't thought about for awhile. Charlotte was a girl John sort of dated right after his mission. She was three years younger than him and one of his sister's best friends. Charlotte and John's sister Hope had been friends for a couple of years. Her family was from Laguna Beach and Hope met her at EFY. That same EFY was the first time John saw Charlotte too. John was the cool, older brother, so Charlotte was enamored with him immediately. He knew he was blessed to have four sisters. They taught him lessons everyday on how to treat and communicate with women. But the best lesson he learned was how to pamper women and still have control of the relationship.

Hope was three years younger and his other sister Melody was two years older. John had a very extensive dating pool growing up, composed of older women and younger women. To his sister's friends he was the cute older brother and the sweet, innocent younger brother.

At EFY John was cool. He hung out with the cool crowd and even did something really cool at the talent show. He was a hip guy. John was also smart. He learned from his mother to never burn a bridge so while he was around any of his sister's friends he was very nice to his sisters. Charlotte took notice of John from a far and he knew it. He thought it was flattering but nothing more.

As time went on, Charlotte was always there. She went to John's missionary farewell and waved goodbye to him as he got onto the plane. While he was out there in Brazil, she even wrote to him half a dozen times, which was more than most of the people John knew.

John had always liked Charlotte but that was it. The day he returned home from his mission he saw the banners, the balloons, his brothers and sisters, Mom and Dad, and there she was too. Charlotte.

John was released from his mission and went through the traditional strange "I think I'm still a missionary phase" and "I'm kind of a nerd phase." He knew he had to shake that sentiment fast, so he went to a Young Adult dance with Hope and Charlotte. Now back in the day, Young Adult dances in Southern California were the bomb. John had sweet memories of those dances and what transpired those sweaty nights in the packed cultural halls up and down the California coast.

He walked out onto the dance floor with Charlotte and Hope in tow. Before his mission, John was the king at these dances. He knew everyone and had dance moves that brought the spotlight to him. Now it was a different story. He danced with no rhythm. That first dance after his mission was a painful night for John in that respect but on the flipside of the coin it was also a great night of discovery.

John looked at Charlotte with different eyes. She was no longer the little girl he remembered. Now she was almost a woman. And the way she looked at him, it was so hard to resist looking back at her. Charlotte had "the glow." She was living righteously, doing her thing, and she was happy. John liked that about her, beautiful and happy. What a sweet combination.

He danced up a storm that night with his pathetic rhythm, reached exhaustion and headed outside to cool off and get some fresh air. He looked up at the stars all around him. He thought about his mission and all he had done in Brazil and then he knew he definitely needed to get things moving. He needed to make the transition into life after the mission.

John was all alone outside with just his thoughts when he was interrupted. It was Charlotte.

"Hi," she said with her sweet innocent voice.

"Hey. It was hot in there." John tried to play it cool.

"Yeah. I know. The A/C probably isn't on."

"You having a good time, Charlotte?"

"Yeah. Are you?" she returned with a vibrant smile.

"Yeah. I'm just trying to adjust. The music has changed and stuff. Except for 'White Lines,' they still play that song and I have no idea why." John's cool conversation skills were missing as well.

Charlotte sang a verse from the song. "White lines. Freeze. Rock."

"Nice to know some things don't change." They both shared a laugh.

Charlotte searched for what she really wanted to say. "Did you get my letters?" "Yeah. Sorry I only wrote you back once or twice." John remembered almost every word from every letter. Charlotte was good with words.

"That's okay. I knew you were really busy. So, what are you going to do now?"

She really wanted him to say something about the letters or the care package she sent him.

John knew it was the question of the hour and then he thought about "The Plan."

"I'm going to BYU and major in business." he said.

"Cool. I'm starting there in the fall."

"So, you're going to be there and so am I. That's cool." John put two and two together.

"Do you know where you're going to live?"

John realized he didn't have it all figured out. "No. I have no idea where I'm going to live." He couldn't help but laugh.

Charlotte joined him as they both laughed side by side on that clear night.

"I'm glad you're back." Charlotte put her hand on his shoulder.

John immediately felt something, like electricity shooting through his body. "Thank you," he said.

He looked into Charlotte's eyes, her face closer to his, inches away, their eyes locked onto each other, as they moved closer and even closer yet.

"Boy, it's hot in there," Hope said sucking in air. "What are you guys doing?" John and Charlotte had already distanced themselves from each other. "I just got here. John, how long have you been out here?" Charlotte responded.

"Only a couple of minutes. It feels good out here." He started to catch on.

"You okay?" Hope looked at him searching.

"I'm good."

"Your face is a little flushed. Are you sure?" Hope wanted to hear something more.

John gave the typical RM answer, "I'm just trying to adapt. It's been awhile."

"Come on. There's some really cute guys I want you to meet." Hope grabbed Charlotte by the arm and lead her away.

"I'll see you guys in there," he said hoping she'd stay. Charlotte looked back at John.

After the dance, the cool thing to do was to go to Denny's or to a little place down on PCH called Harbor House that was open 24 hours. And as always a group of people was going to the Harbor House. John asked Hope if she wanted to go but she was pretty much over the night.

"Do you want to go?" Hope wanted to make sure Charlotte was taken care of.

"I don't know." Charlotte waited to hear what John was doing.

"I think I'm going to go. I need to get out there and socialize." He wanted to see what Charlotte would do.

"Great. If you want to go Charlotte, you can go with John and I'll just get a ride home from someone else." Hope was oblivious to the chemistry between them. She was tired and had to wake up early the next day, an act of destiny.

"Yeah. I think I'll go to the Harbor House too." Charlotte

smiled. She knew it'd just be her and John.

She sat in the car next to John. It was painfully quiet.

"I don't really want to go to the Harbor House," John said, breaking the silence.

"Okay. Why don't we drive around." She didn't care. The Harbor House was an excuse to spend time with him.

Charlotte and John drove around for at least an hour in that slightly uncomfortable silence with each of them stealing glances every once and awhile.

"Turn here. Yeah. Right here. We can park right there. And then we walk down to the ocean." Charlotte decided to take charge. She told John it was a place they could talk.

Charlotte led the way. They walked down wooden steps to a cove right by the water.

"Right here. Isn't it beautiful?" Charlotte was happy with herself.

John looked around. It was beautiful, and peaceful too. "Yeah. It's nice."

"Sit down." She sat down without a care in the world.

"Right." John was awkward. He plopped down next to Charlotte. He looked around, the clear night, stars a plenty, and a beautiful woman at his side. John was so nervous, like it was the first time he had ever sat next to a girl in his entire life.

"So, did you have a fun time tonight?"

"You asked me that already," Charlotte said with a smile and a tap on his arm.

The touch of her hand startled him a little and he jumped.

"You're right, I did. I have to be honest with you. I'm just kind of awkward right now." John's foot was in his mouth.

"Don't worry. I won't tell anyone." Charlotte laughed lightly.

John looked at this girl, now a woman, a smart, funny, and beautiful woman. Her eyes gleamed at him.

Charlotte took in a breath and moved closer to John. John started to feel that same electric sensation, and it grew as Charlotte moved even closer to him. Her hands rested on his shoulders, his whole body felt it now.

He was drawn in, his face moved toward hers. John could feel her breath on his lips. Maybe it was the strawberry smack-lips he'd remembered her wearing. It was sweet like nectar. He moved even closer to Charlotte. Their lips inched toward each other, centimeters, milli-meters, and finally —"we have lift off." Their lips touched, an innocent and soft contact.

Whoa! he thought as he pulled away.

Charlotte looked at him again, with that look, the look that could enslave any man for eternity.

John moved back next to Charlotte and they kissed again, slowly and tenderly. Their lips stayed connected as if Super Glue bonded them and then he pulled away again.

"I'm sorry. I don't know if we should be doing this." John tried to find reason in it all.

"Okay." Charlotte wanted to hear something else.

"You're my sister's best friend and I don't want to give you the wrong idea. I mean, I kissed you and I wanted to kiss you, but you're my sister's best friend and if this never worked out then you'd feel awkward coming over to my house and hanging out with Hope and then I'd feel weird that you feel weird. And it would just be weird." John desperately put together his case.

"It would be weird. I get it." Charlotte understood but she wanted to kiss again.

"I don't want to just kiss all of my sister's friends." Once again John said the wrong thing.

"Then you've kissed your sister's friends before?" Charlotte tried to pinpoint his reasoning. She knew if she kept at it, they could be kissing again instead of talking.

"Yeah. But that was a long time ago." John was a changed

man; at least he thought he was.

"Well, don't worry about it 'cause I kissed you." Charlotte stood up and brushed the sand off her jeans. Charlotte looked over at John, "What time is it?"

"I'd better take you home." John looked down at his watch; it was late, way past his ten o'clock curfew. But he wasn't on a mission anymore—*man, I need help.*

After that night on the beach John and Charlotte remained friends. They crossed paths frequently at BYU. Charlotte called John to tell him about her dating adventures and for advice on men.

John called to fill her in on his latest relationship but more than anything John liked to hear Charlotte's voice. He enjoyed talking to her and sometimes that's hard to come by.

"Charlotte Lee." John thought about her deeply. *What if I had actually tried to see what could've happened after that night?*

Pete and Brandy continued to dance cheek to cheek. What a perfect couple. While they were engaged Brandy let Pete play his Sega DreamCast with the boys and Pete appeased Brandy by going to a chick flick with her every once once in a while. Pete and Brandy and everyone on the dance floor had stopped dancing and all eyes were on John.

There was only one reason for that. John opened the CD player and slid another CD in, it worked, and the dancing continued. Pete stared over at John. John gave him the universal "I'm sorry bro" sign and that was that.

John prepped the next CD when a familiar voice sparked his interest. He looked up to see Brother and Sister Lee.

Sister Lee was one of the coolest people John had ever met. She had seven kids, her Doctorate Degree in History, Relief Society president, and a member of the California State Senate. "John. Is that you?"

"Hey. How are you guys doing?" John said.

Brother Lee wasn't a slouch either. He was a successful patent attorney who, for a hobby, invented random gizmos. Brother Lee also played in the big leagues for a couple of years for the Anaheim Angels. "I told you it was him," Brother Lee said with a smile.

"So, what are you guys doing here?" John responded quickly, hoping to hear about Charlotte.

"We know Brandy's parents. We all go way back to our college days at BYU."

"Way back. Way back. If you know what I mean, John," Brother Lee interjected.

Sister Lee said, "And what's new with you?" She was one of those people who asked questions because she honestly cared about you.

"Just working, paying my dues to the corporate world," John said with a matter of fact attitude.

"The indentured servant days. I remember that time. We all have to go through it."

Out of all of the people in the world, the Lees were the last people John had expected to see. Only one thing kept crossing John's mind.

"And how's Charlotte?"

"She's doing fine." Sister Lee knew John would ask that question.

"She just got engaged," Brother Lee followed close behind with a smile.

Stop time. John's face dropped, "Engaged?" His head felt like it was going to explode.

CHAPTER 3

Phil Collins had a great song in the eighties, not when he went solo but when he was part of the extremely talented Genesis.

The song he was remembering was "Throwing It All Away." That song echoed in his head. John couldn't remember how the song started or even a single verse but the chorus he couldn't ever forget.

He sang the chorus with bravado. "Throwing It All Away. Throwing It All Away. Throwing It All Away. Throwing It All Away."

John had no clue why that particular song decided to consume his brain at that moment. He hadn't listened to that song for a very long time.

Phil Collins songs are weird like that. You'll be going about your day and then all of the sudden you're singing "Invisible Touch." Phil's music had some bizarre mind control capability to it. John had heard from someone that they blared "Invisible Touch" from the air during the Gulf War. Or maybe it wasn't Phil Collins at all—possibly it was Elton John's "Your Song." John knew it was someone British and someone who was short.

"Throwing It All Away." That was a great song. John was tired of thinking about Phil Collins. He had more important things to pontificate about.

John sat alone on the edge of his bed staring into the mirror on the sliding closet door. He pushed Phil Collins completely out of his mind and thought about what had transpired the night before. John played the scene over and over again where Brother and Sister Lee told him that their daughter Charlotte was engaged. He was still dumbfounded. His mind was racing:

Why was I thinking about Charlotte when this happened? What were Charlotte's parents doing there? Has Charlotte ever thought about me? Is pontificating the greatest word in the English language? John asked himself question after question hoping to find some kind of comfort, that it was all a coincidence. *She's engaged. She's taken. Should I send a gift? Should I go to the wedding? Should I call her?* John only added more and more fuel to the fire of questions. He wanted it to be cut and dry. But it wasn't. Hearing the news that Charlotte was engaged should've made John's decision to move on easier, but in fact it complicated everything even more.

He was still thinking of more options about the time his alarm went off at 7 a.m.

He stood up and walked into the bathroom and started his morning ritual. John had actually remembered to buy toothpaste. The day was starting off well. Fridays were always John's favorite day of the week. He couldn't remember ever missing a Friday at work. The office was a more relaxed, calm setting, and most of his co-workers dressed down—no suits or ties.

John couldn't get Charlotte out of his head. He put some water in his mouth and swallowed and then he realized he was supposed to rinse.

"Oh well, I hope toothpaste won't hurt you. What does it have in it anyway?" John read the box. Fluoride. And what else? How about water, hydrated silica, glycerin orbital and sodium saccharin? Hey, that's got sugar in it. Who would've known." He was talking to himself out loud. John put down the tube of toothpaste. He liked to find out what was in everything. He knew fluoride was in there and he also knew he was going to live.

He tried to keep himself occupied with anything because any time there was a free moment he started to think about Charlotte.

"What is Charlotte doing right now?" John couldn't keep her out. In fact, the night before he dreamed about her. Most of the dream was fuzzy but Charlotte was definitely in it. He remembered her smiling at him. What a great smile she had, John mused, as the thought of Charlotte possessed him again.

John went into his room. It was time to get ready for work. He dreaded that part of his day. In less than an hour he'd be sitting in his tiny cubicle punching numbers. Unless. . . John picked up the phone and dialed a number from memory.

"Hello Bill. It's John Edwards." John coughed and then continued. "Yeah. I'm feeling under the weather. I don't know. I must've come down with something."

"The flu is going around," Bill said in a matter-of-fact tone.

John let out another convincing and contagious cough. "Yeah. I think it's better if I stay in bed all day and try to fight it off." John was all smiles. He had checked with the office manager; he had four sick days left and a week of vacation. Now he only had three sick days left.

"Thanks Bill. Oh, I will get plenty of rest. Yeah. I know. I'll drink lots of liquids." John said goodbye and finally hung up the phone.

John felt guilty for lying to his boss, but he just needed a day off. "He was an Eagle Scout and was taught to be trust-worthy, loyal, helpful, friendly, courteous, kind, obedient, something, something, and something." He hadn't thought about the Scout Law since his fourteenth birthday at his Eagle Court of Honor. In John's family you had to get your Eagle before you could get your driver's license, so John got it early. His brother Josh didn't get his license until he was seventeen.

John did have a little headache. More than anything he needed the day off to recharge his battery and to clear his head. The phone sat there beckoning John to pick it up. And so he did and called Southwest Airlines. They had a special during the week to Salt Lake City.

"Why not." John was on his way .

He had to do something drastic or otherwise he'd be thinking about Charlotte for the rest of the year.

Why do certain women have the power to do this to me? John thought as he paid the taxi driver. The airport wasn't busy and John decided to take an early flight. He sat down at his departure gate and waited.

Now he started to have second thoughts: *How pathetic can you be? What will this trip do for ya, huh? Are you even going to have the courage to approach Charlotte?* John's mind talked too much. Sometimes John thought his mind was tough on him. John's sister Hope was living in Provo. He'd go visit her, thus validating his trip to Provo. To see Charlotte was only a secondary reason for flying up there; at least John tried to convince himself of that.

John pulled a book out of his carry-on. He started to read. He decided he would immerse himself in the characters and the world the author of the book had created. John read one sentence and then he read the same sentence again, and again and again. Who was he fooling? He couldn't concentrate. It was no use. Charlotte had officially commandeered his brain and he was merely along for the ride.

He started to run different scenarios in his head. *What if Charlotte is dumbfounded when she sees me? What if Charlotte isn't happy at all with her fiancé? Yeah. She realizes she's just settling for him. What if Charlotte has never been able to forget me or that 'kiss' on the beach? Or what if Charlotte has totally forgotten about me and moved on?*

John stopped dead in his tracks. "How did that last thought get in my head? It was all positive and then. Of course she remembers me. I'm her best friend's handsome older brother. She'll never be able to forget me. And that 'kiss.' I still can't forget that 'kiss.' There's no way she won't remember it.' John was torturing himself. 'You're thinking too much. Shut up brain."

That was the biggest problem of all. John knew how his brain worked. He knew it would never stop thinking and as long as it did there would always be a hint of doubt. What if he was completely wrong? And at a weak moment in his life he tried to make up something that wasn't there at all. The truth. John was lonely. He'd had a couple of girlfriends over the years but nothing serious. Out of all his friends everybody knew he'd be the last one to get married. And everyone was right.

The first class passengers started to board the plane. John knew he had only a few more minutes to decide. He could walk away and just laugh off the whole situation and go on with his life.

"All rows, once again I repeat we are now boarding all rows for Flight #177 direct to Salt Lake City." The loud speaker stopped as travelers lined up at the door. John stood up and picked up his carry-on. He looked over at the door and then anywhere else. He looked down at his watch. John had to make his move. It was a long excruciating process with baby steps leading the way but he made it to the flight attendant at the door. *What's the worst that could happen?*

CHAPTER 4

What's the worst that could happen? In hindsight John realized that was possibly the worst question he could ask himself. The question triggered a story he had heard from a friend about some guy they knew who had a similar situation.

The Guy who John's friend referred to as just "Guy" had graduated from BYU and then accepted a sweet offer from one of the "Big Three" accounting firms. His offer was from Deloitte and Touch in their Los Angeles office. At the time, Guy had been dating a beautiful, cool girl, "a catch." And Guy was starting to fall for her but he couldn't pass up the career opportunity. The Girl was a junior so she had another year at the Y. Guy moved to L.A. and said goodbye to this spectacular girl with the promise that they'd see each other frequently.

Months passed by, four months total. Guy kept his promise and flew up to Salt Lake twice a month during that time. But Guy couldn't take it anymore. He had to be by his girl, so he quit his job, packed up his stuff, and drove back up to Provo. It was snowing hard when Guy arrived at the girl's door. Guy knocked on the door holding a bouquet of sunflowers and Gerber daisies. He waited with a giant smile on his face.

His girl answered the door but something was missing. She didn't have the same "Glad to see you" smile on her face, more like a look of confusion or "What are you doing here?" And that was when the girl told Guy that she had met someone and they were dating seriously.

Guy wanted to bury himself in the snow. The girl told Guy that she didn't have the heart to tell him earlier. Guy's smile faded.

"Do you need to put that in the overhead?" John looked at the flight attendant. She was older, probably traveled the world twice over, and she was courteous and good at her job. He knew she truly enjoyed her line of work. *That's fascinating. Serving people on planes all day. I guess someone looks at this as his or her dream job.* He lifted his bag over his head, "Thank you. I'll put it in the overhead compartment."

John didn't know if the story about Guy was true or if it was "Mormon Folklore." Mormons loved to hypothesize. One of John's favorite Mormon folklore stories was that Michael Jackson had joined the church. The man who created the moonwalk, who wore the diamond glove, who became whiter every decade, who couldn't stay out of the headlines, had inevitably joined the church—that was "Mormon Folklore."

He convinced himself that the story about Guy was simply some story somebody made up. He gave a sigh of relief and sat down next to a young man in a brand new suit, starched white shirt, and a brand new scripture bag on his lap. It was obvious to John that this young man was on his way to the MTC. He'd been there and done that and now reminisced about how short the flight from L.A. to Salt Lake was.

The young man looked around trying to get a bearing on the people around him. John looked right at him.

"I hope it's a quick flight. I'm John. How are you?" John extended his hand to Elder Palmer opening the conversation.

"Jared. I mean Elder Palmer." Elder Palmer wasn't used to his new name quite yet.

"So what is it? Jared or Elder Palmer?"

"My real name is Jared but for the next two years I'll have the title of Elder Palmer." Elder Palmer returned with a standard answer.

"Oh. Are you one of those missionary guys?" John was going to have a little fun with the young missionary.

"Yes. I'm a representative of The Church of Jesus Christ of Latter-day Saints or the Mormons. Right now I'm heading to Provo, Utah, to the Missionary Training Center. I will be trained as a missionary and learn Spanish and then spend almost two years in the Barcelona, Spain Mission." Elder Palmer jumped at the opportunity to talk about the church.

No duh! That's what John wanted to say. He decided he was going to make Elder Palmer's day.

"Barcelona, Spain. Wow. You are going to have a good time. I had a friend in high school who was Mormon. His name was Michael Smith. Do you know him?" John had to play the "Mormon Name Game." And Michael Smith was a perfect Mormon name to play the game with.

Anytime you met another Mormon you had to ask them if they knew a particular person. Most of the time, actually ninety-nine times out of a hundred the answer was, "No. I don't know them." And then that would be followed by, "Well. I had to ask you anyway."

"Where did you go to high school?" Elder Palmer leaned over to John.

John had to think quickly, "Westwood High."

"No. I don't know Michael Smith. Did you ever go to church with him or to any activities, like a dance, something like that?" Elder Palmer searched his memory banks.

John was impressed Elder Palmer was building a firm relationship of trust. He thought Elder Palmer was a natural. "Elder Palmer would make a great missionary."

He had to put his thoughts together. *No. He never went to church with his friend Michael Smith but one time he went to a dance.*

John looked over at Elder Palmer who was waiting with anticipation.

"I went to a dance once. I think there was over six hundred people or so and I also remember there were some really beautiful girls."

"Yeah. The dances were great. It was a nice, clean atmosphere to have fun and meet new friends and spend time with old friends," Elder Palmer said and smiled. The kid was really good.

And that was when it all changed. Elder Palmer reached into his carry-on under his seat and pulled out a Book of Mormon with the dark blue cover and gold writing.

John knew this book well. Although when he served his mission he gave away "O Livro de Mormon," but it was all the same.

Elder Palmer started to open up the Book of Mormon to Third Nephi and talked about when Christ appeared to the people on the American continent. Elder Palmer must've gotten his hands on the discussions from an older brother who had already served a mission. Before long Elder Palmer was inviting John to prevail himself of the promise in Moroni 10: 3-5 that he would know the book was true through the Holy Ghost. *What a trip*, John thought.

John had two choices. Either he could tell Elder Palmer he was already a member of the Church and that he was only burning time on the flight or he could go on with the charade. John contemplated that choice as Elder Palmer handed the Book of Mormon over to John.

"And I put my testimony at the front about how I feel about this book and how it's changed my life." Elder Palmer handed the book proudly to John.

John knew the choice he had to make. This kid had put his heart and soul in his desire to be a missionary at all times and in all places, even before he entered the MTC. John would have to do the right thing at that moment. So, John took the Book of Mormon and thanked Elder Palmer for the gift.

"I'll read it." John would read the Book of Mormon and he would give that Book of Mormon to someone else.

Elder Palmer was on cloud nine. He had just had his first real missionary experience. What a great story he had to tell his fellow missionaries and instructors in the MTC.

John looked down at the Book of Mormon and started to feel a little guilty for misrepresenting himself to Elder Palmer. But it was too late now and Elder Palmer had a permanent smile on his face that was priceless. He knew it was wrong to do what he did but he also knew Elder Palmer would never forget that plane flight.

A flight when he, a young missionary on his way to the MTC, sat down next to a stranger and talked to him about the gospel. It's funny how things work out. *That was me eight years ago,* John laughed inside. Deep down he knew his stretching of the truth would catch up to him.

John walked from the plane with his mind racing again. *Where did the time go? What have I done? What have I become since my mission?* John reminisced about his college graduation and then the post-graduation trip to Europe with his brother backpacking for four months. He thought about the couple of months when he was an extra for "Beverly Hills, 90210," and one particular New Year's Eve episode when he was front and center doing the cabbage patch.

It wasn't all bad. He had some good relationships, some pretty good relationships. He had even dated a completely insane, mental chick. She loved Star Trek and had a cat named "Tabby." Now that was awful.

At every turn John had been able to weather the storm and either learn from the situation or just laugh at himself.

John put down his carry-on next to the Hertz Rent-A-Car desk. *Man, this thing is heavy. What'd you put in here?* John was talking to himself again. He was met by a happy-go-lucky blonde, about twenty or so, probably from Richfield or some other small town in Utah. He guessed that because she had the "I lived on a farm hairdo" with enough hairspray on her bangs to fight gravity. Her name was Cassie. "How can I help you sir?" Cassie threw John her golden smile.

He could already sense a different attitude in the air. He knew Cassie genuinely wanted to help him. She was sincere and there were no strings attached. Living in L.A. had made John a little jaded. Too often he had met people who presented themselves as the "salt of earth" and turned out to be vultures with ulterior motives—maybe not vultures but had ulterior motives just the same. That was L.A.—Dog-eat-Dog then that Dog would eat the littlest Dog around and so forth.

Now John was in Happy Valley. He felt good to be able to speak to someone and not to have to worry where the conversation was going.

"Yes Cassie, I would like a mid-size car. John Edwards. I have a reservation." He handed her his confirmation form. "Just one moment John." Cassie was multi-tasked, as she showed by answering the phone, taking care of John, and pointing a nice elderly couple to where they could find Gate 34. He watched Cassie at work.

Cassie looked up at John. He smiled back: *I wonder what kind of men Cassie likes? Maybe if she did something different with her hair and bought a whole new wardrobe, then she wouldn't be half bad.* Sometimes he was too judgmental.

He knew people probably ripped on him too, so he didn't feel that horrible. John was deep in thought. He tried to stop thinking about Cassie because he knew desperation was starting to set in. Everything was beginning to look attractive to him. Cassie was a nice girl and all. She even hooked him up with unlimited mileage. Maybe she did feel a little something towards John. Of course the last thought drove him to think about Charlotte.

Charlotte was to be the standard whereby all women were to be measured for the rest of his life. That thought made John return to the past and his optimum remembrance of Charlotte and the kiss on the beach.

CHAPTER 5

It was a quick drive south on I-15 down to Provo. John thought he'd kill two birds with one stone. His sister Hope lived on Y Mountain and had a two-year old named Luke. He'd visit Hope and Luke and get Charlotte's whereabouts. It was perfect.

Hope met and married her husband at BYU as most Mormons do when they go to school at BYU? Once again John started to feel retarded. *What was his problem? He graduated from BYU. Did he make some mistake? Was he cursed? Why didn't he meet someone and marry while at BYU?* John knew he was hard on himself but his father taught him it would make him a stronger and greater man. John felt like he'd had enough. He wanted to be in love.

His sister Hope was sort of the opposite of John. She went to BYU with no plan at all, except to graduate with some kind of degree. And life just happened.

Hope met Nathan, a pre-med student, her junior year. They dated for three months and got married shortly after. After the honeymoon they received a surprise. Hope was pregnant— Honeymoon Instant Family.

And now two years later Hope was still in Provo and Nathan was graduating in the summer. Hope wouldn't think of leaving Luke with a babysitter so she had discontinued her education for the time being. Now Hope had a small day care during the day watching other poor students' kids.

John pulled up to the infamous Y Mountain. He knew he was there because in front of him was the traffic of mothers pushing strollers along the sidewalks.

Hope liked John and vice versa. Growing up they had the typical fights and arguments over what to watch on TV or when to roll the car window up because it was too cold outside, but for the most part they had a great relationship.

It was quiet as John stood outside of Hope's condo (if you could call it a condo). John knocked on the door anyway. Then he knocked again. He could hear the sound of little feet running full speed for the door. The door opened and five toddlers, including Luke, stared up at John. "Hi guys. I'm John." Luke smiled up at him.

The other toddlers ran after each other playing some kind of game only young children understand. Hope walked around the corner. John put his arms out, "Surprise."

"What are you doing here?" Hope walked over to John and gave him a hug.

Hope wanted to hear everything about John's life. He had forgotten how she loved to talk. He looked around and noticed they were alone.

"Are you sure you can talk right now? What about all of the kids?"

"I put on *Blues Clues*. They'll all be quiet for about an hour. We have plenty of time."

Now John had heard it all. "What? A video? I can't believe you did that. You said you'd never sit your kids down in front of the TV. What's happened to you?"

"That was before I had a kid. TV entertainment gives me time. It's a blessing. Come with me," Hope said. She had changed.

She led John into the TV room where all of the toddlers were sitting on the carpet watching *Blues Clues*. And more importantly they were quiet and behaving. John and Hope walked back into the kitchen.

"So, how long are you going to be here?"

"Did you see their eyes? Those kids are being brainwashed right now by a little blue dog and that includes my nephew Luke. His eyes were glued to the TV." John couldn't get that image out of his head. He smiled at Hope.

"So, how long are you here?" Hope wanted to find out why he came to Provo.

"Probably today and tomorrow. Why?"

John could see it coming down the tracks before Hope even started to talk. "There's this cute girl I want to set you up with." He had heard this before from those same lips. He'd been out on dates with some of "Hope's cute girls."

Six months earlier John was set up with Barbara and, to put it nicely, she wasn't his type. Physical attraction was very important to John. The first thing Hope said to John when she saw him was, "Do you think you'll go out with Barbara again?"

John looked her straight in the face and gave her an emphatic "No." And then she said, "Stop being so picky John. You're never going to find anyone good enough for you."

His family always labeled him as "not knowing what he wanted," or "wanting the wrong kind of girl" or their most used clique, "being too picky."

"Maybe I'll go out with your friend the next time I'm down. So, what else is going on?" He looked up at Hope trying to avoid the potential train wreck.

"What do you mean?" Hope was confused.

"You know. . . have you seen anybody lately that we know?" John went fishing again.

Hope again was not on the same page. "Who might you be talking about?"

John had to spin it. "I don't know. Anything going on with people we both know that are good friends of yours."

"I have no idea what you're talking about, John."

John was tired of being sneaky and used another tactic. He

just blurted it out. "Charlotte Lee. What's going on with her?"

"The latest?" Hope wasn't sure what he wanted to hear.

"Yes. The latest."

Hope started to put together everything she'd heard about Charlotte. "Well, she's engaged."

"Engaged. No way. Are you serious?" John tried to fake his response.

"Yeah. I think she's getting married in, like, six months." John shook his head, hammed it up a bit, "Charlotte. Huh. How weird is that?"

"So, why are you here?" Hope was starting to sense something.

"I have to visit a client in Salt Lake." John was quick on the defensive.

"I didn't know you had any clients in Salt Lake."

"You're right. I don't have any clients here. I actually have a job interview." John had forgotten how detail-oriented his sister was.

"When?"

"Tomorrow." John responded without thinking.

"Yeah. But tomorrow is Saturday. Do they do interviews on Saturday?"

John was starting to dig himself a hole. He wanted to tell Hope the truth, that he had come for the sole purpose of spending a day with Charlotte. John just wanted the opportunity to see Charlotte and then rely on his heart for the "Yes" or "No" to pursue her. Hope would think John was crazy, so he couldn't tell her just then.

"You're right. Most companies don't do interviews on Saturday. But this particular company has made an exception due to my circumstances." He answered Hope's next question with another little white lie.

"What company is it?" Hope wanted more.

"It doesn't matter. It's the first interview. Should we go check on the kids?" John tried desperately to end it.

"We still have a good fifteen minutes." Hope looked down at her watch.

"Well, I better get going," John stood up. He wanted out.

Hope stood up too and they hugged. She truly cared about John's happiness and wanted him to know that. Hope said, "It was good to see you John. You look good."

She escorted John to the door past all of the toddlers watching *Blues Clues*. "They're all being brainwashed by that weird-looking blue dog. Look at them. You should try to play that tape backwards, just in case."

Hope laughed.

"Take care, Luke," John said and patted him on the head. Luke kept his eyes glued to the TV.

"If you stay longer you better come back for dinner and visit us." Hope opened the front door. John took a step outside the door and then stopped.

"Do you happen to have Charlotte's phone number? I was thinking I should congratulate her," John stated nonchalantly as the door started to close.

For the first time during their whole conversation, Hope became super-quiet.

John was quick to add, "Is that cool?"

"Sure," Hope returned, still a little fazed. She went back into the kitchen and returned with just the thing John needed most of all, Charlotte's number.

He took the number, gave Hope a kiss on the cheek and was off.

John hurried to his rental car. Everything was working out so perfectly. It was then, as he started his car, that he had a moment of truth. He was bombarded with every possible negative thought about Charlotte rejecting him.

He sat there for a time in the parking lot at Y Mountain and took a couple of deep breaths. He had made it this far already and all he had to do now was call up Charlotte and set up a meeting. It was that easy. John finally swallowed his pride and the self-doubt left him.

CHAPTER 6

The nearest pay phone was around the corner. John almost forgot to put his car in park—he was so excited to call Charlotte. His car started to roll backward and he quickly slammed it into park.

John held the number in his hand. It all felt good. It all felt right. His hand began to tremble a little but he chalked it up to nerves. He put the receiver to his ear and dialed the number with lighting speed.

"It's ringing," John said out loud. The phone rang again and again. Every time was more excruciating for him.

He was about to hang up when he heard a soft, gentle voice, "Hello?"

"Hi." John put the receiver back to his ear.

"Who is this?" Charlotte asked curiously. Her caller ID couldn't verify the number.

"You wouldn't believe me if I told you." John tried to make some sense of what he had to say.

"What?"

"It's John Edwards. You know, Hope's older brother. Remember?" John grimaced. He wished he had been more articulate.

"John? No way. Of course I remember you. How are you? What are you doing?"

He had opened the door. "It's funny you asked. I'm in Provo. I have some business in Salt Lake, an interview."

"Which one? Business or an interview?" Charlotte was sharp.

"A business interview," John came right back. He couldn't have an awkward moment.

"Oh. That's nice."

"So, I'll only be in town today and tomorrow. I was thinking we could get together for lunch or something." There, he said it.

"Lunch?" Charlotte thought. *Where did that come from?*

"Are you busy the next couple of days?" John tried to act oblivious to what he knew was true.

"No. Yes. Did Hope tell you anything?"

"No. Was she supposed to tell me something?" Of course Hope told him and her parents too—he didn't care. He had to see her.

"I got engaged last week," Charlotte blurted out, just like her dad had.

"Engaged. No way. Are you serious? Well, congratulations. Now we have two things to talk about," John replied with the same fake surprise. To hear Charlotte say it, however, ate him up inside.

"That doesn't bother you?" Charlotte was confused.

John knew it bothered him. It struck a chord of jealousy inside of him. "Where do you want to meet?"

"Oh, I don't know," Charlotte replied apprehensively.

John cut in, "That's my other line. I have to get it. So, pick a place."

Charlotte didn't know why but she said, "Buona Vita on Center Street at three p.m. tomorrow."

"See you there." John quickly hung up. A big mischievous smile formed on his face. She was going to see him.

John pumped his fist up into the air celebrating his first victory in a while. It felt amazing.

Everything had to be perfect, the setting, the lighting, the atmosphere, the food, and even the waiter. John stood patiently in front of a young hostess with rosy cheeks. The hostess flashed a smile, "Can I help you?"

"Hi, I have a reservation at three o'clock."

"First name please." The hostess responded robotically.

"It should be under Charlotte for two."

The hostess followed her finger down the reservation book. "Here it is. You're a little early."

"Who's your best waiter?" John couldn't be distracted.

"We don't call them waiters. We call them servers." The hostess was polite about it.

John smiled but really wanted to say, *You could call them Sally for all I care.*

"Who's your best server?" John hoped he'd said the magic words.

The hostess replied quickly, "Paul."

"Great."

"No wait. Paul doesn't come on until four o'clock."

"Could Paul come in earlier?" John could tell the hostess wasn't the sharpest tool in the shed.

"No. Paul had class on Saturday."

"Do you have someone else as good as Paul?"

"Kurt's actually really good too." The hostess was happy to provide an answer. "Kurt. Great. That solves everything. Can I have Kurt wait on me at three o'clock?"

"First, I have to tell him that someone has requested him."

"Just do this. Tell Kurt it will be worth his while." John was starting to lose his patience.

And with that John walked around the restaurant looking for the best table. He shouted from across the other side of the restaurant as he walked back to the hostess, "I want that table."

"We'll try to make it perfect. Are you proposing to someone tonight?" The hostess took note and smiled as John met her eye to eye again.

"No, she's already engaged," he smirked and headed out the door, putting his fate in the hands of the young hostess.

CHAPTER 7

Charlotte stood in front of her vanity full-length mirror. She looked down at her watch. It read 2:45pm. She looked absolutely stunning. The years had been extremely kind to her. She had grown two inches since the last time John had seen her. A 5'11" vision of beauty with genetics that would make most girls hate her by just looking at her. She was as close to perfect without being perfect as anyone could get.

Her style matched her beauty, simple and timeless. Charlotte had on some hip-hugger red-washed Diesel jeans and a black DKNY sweater. She was ready to go, but her face wore a concerned look.

Charlotte knew she could not just show up and that would be the end of it. Deep down, however, she wanted to see if she still felt anything for John. That phone call on the previous day had caught her completely off guard.

She was busy that Friday afternoon sifting through bridal magazines, trying to decide on the one wedding dress she'd wear to the temple to be married in for time and all eternity. As she turned the pages her thoughts went to Brian—that was her fiancé. She thought about the children they would have and their life together. Charlotte had already compiled a list of names for her future children. Over the years she'd narrowed the list down to names for five girls and five boys. She wasn't thinking about having ten kids, maybe more like six, but it never hurt to have some alternative choices just in case another sibling took one of her names for one of their offspring.

Charlotte had met Brian Jenkins through a friend on a

blind date. Brian wasn't exactly her type. He was a good-looking guy who had been awarded the Hinckley scholarship. He was also very grounded. He had a stable future ahead of him in the corporate finance world. He had already been accepted to graduate school at the Harvard Business School like his father and grandfather before him.

Brian's style was more East Coast, always sporting The Gap, Abercrombie and Fitch, or some other present day yuppie brand.

Brian wasn't boring. He was just mature. At least, that's what Charlotte told her roommates after they asked her why she liked him. And Brian was fun, not like wild or off-the-wall at times but fun. In fact, the whole time Brian and Charlotte had dated, not once had they had a pillow fight, wrestled each other in the grass, smashed a snowball in each other's face, or gone clubbing to freak with each other on the dance floor.

He was by the book romantically. There were no surprises, no drama, no mixed signals, and absolutely no spontaneity. She always wondered about that "spark" or "electricity" she'd felt with other guys, especially with John Edwards.

Charlotte nonetheless liked Brian for several reasons. Brian was kind, generous, smart, giving, a good listener, had a great testimony of the restored gospel, came from a great family, and lastly, wasn't a jerk. She had dated a lot of guys at BYU and was quite popular. She had dated guys from the star All-American quarterback to the ASB President to the semi-pro snowboarder to the wannabe rock star. She'd dated them all. Brian was the first guy who really respected her. And Charlotte was tired of being a "booty call," or dealing with unfaithful boyfriends, or of fickle relationships with no depth or driven merely by physical attraction.

She wanted something more, more stable, more secure. And then Brian came out of nowhere. It was a perfect fit. But she always wondered.

In contrast, John was devilishly handsome, witty, engaging, daring, even at times stupidly dangerous, and a true free spirit. When John was at BYU, he went out with a slew of gorgeous and pursued women. He was quick to move from one girl to another. He respected most of the girls but he liked to kiss them on the first date. John had gone back to his old ways before his mission of making out with random girls. He was the type of guy Charlotte was tired of dating. He was the type of guy roommates envied and frequently said, "Man. He's hot." The question lingered. Had John changed?

Then the phone rang. It was John. At first, Charlotte thought it couldn't be. And then she focused on his voice. That voice. She knew it well. Her cheeks suddenly were flushed and her head felt light.

Her life was going along well. And now the past of uncertainty and indecision was creeping up on her all of a sudden. *Why is he calling me?* she thought as her mind began to picture John in front of her.

Five minutes had passed on Charlotte's watch. She stared into the mirror and said out loud, "Why did he call me? Why not any other time in my life?" Those questions would haunt Charlotte for the rest of her life.

Charlotte took a couple of deep breaths, pulled her jacket off her chair and headed out the door.

CHAPTER 8

John was sitting at the perfect table with the best server at Buona Vita taking the orders. He looked all around, then down at his watch. It read 3 p.m. Just then panic started to set in. She's not coming. He'd noticed a weird tone in her voice. *Had she figured out his devious plan?*

The minutes moved by painfully slow. It seemed like John glanced down at his watch every split second.

Kurt, the best server in the house, asked if John wanted anything to drink.

"I'll wait. Thanks Kurt." He smiled, trying to hide the discomfort.

John knew he'd made a mistake. He sounded desperate on the phone. Or maybe Hope told Charlotte the truth. Something happened and Charlotte wasn't coming. It was tearing John up inside and he didn't know why.

Four years and no contact—yet, Charlotte always had a place in the back of his mind. His watch read 3:30 p.m.

John was man enough to swallow defeat. He stood up as his legs quivered ever so slightly. He took a step toward the front door. Now he took two steps then four steps toward the door. His head hung low because everything had unraveled before him. *What was he thinking? Like it would be that easy.* John was at the point of depression when sunlight entered the restaurant.

He looked up and was met by the glowing smile of Charlotte.

"Leaving already? I heard this place was good." She had a way with words.

"No. I was just getting some exercise. Taking a couple of laps around the restaurant." John had to be witty.

"Where are you sitting?"

Charlotte and John were quick to re-connect. They were at ease conversing with each other. They talked about their families, their careers, and even dipped a little into their dreams and aspirations.

She told John how she'd killed five goldfish in the last month. And it wasn't because she didn't feed them. She feed them too much and they all got bloated and ballooned up and then died.

"Don't ever buy another goldfish. That's my advice." John was at his best.

Charlotte laughed. What a sweet laugh she had. John hadn't heard it in a long time, but as soon as she began to let out her full giggle, it felt like old times.

He realized he liked everything about Charlotte. She was beautiful, smart, funny, caring, living the gospel, and had great style. She was a class act.

They spent two hours catching up as the time flew by.

Kurt, the best server, was getting frustrated because the restaurant was filling up and they were camping at his table. But John and Charlotte didn't care. They were in their own world. They both needed this time to talk and to listen to each other.

Charlotte's cell phone rang and then rang again. John noticed it first, "Do you need to get that?"

"You know I probably should." Charlotte really didn't want to. She looked down at her caller ID. It read BRIAN. "Hey. I'm at Buona Vita having lunch with an old friend of mine."

John started to look around the restaurant. Then he looked at her rock. *Why did that have to be on her finger right now?* He knew they were getting somewhere and then of course

Brian had to call. He wondered if guys had a sixth sense to know when another guy was trying to make a play on their girl-friend. They must.

Charlotte finished, "Yeah. I know. Me too. Bye honey."

She turned off her cell phone and looked up at John. "It was Brian. His parents are in town and they want to talk about the wedding."

"I thought that's who it was." John didn't want to hear his name again.

"So, where were we?"

"Maybe we should call it a day. It was great talking to you." John was getting anxious.

"Sometimes I forget I'm engaged. I told you that already, right?" She smiled genuinely at him.

John laughed a little. "Under different circumstances we could probably talk more."

"That's what I've always liked about you John. You get it. You understand where people are coming from. You're genuine like that."

John was not worthy of that compliment. "Thanks," He had not been honest with Charlotte. He couldn't.

Charlotte stood up, followed by John.

She walked over to him and stuck out her hand and John stuck out his hand too, but they were too close and their hands crossed each other. They had that awkward handshake-hug. The difference in this exchange is that the hug lasted quite a long time. Then both John and Charlotte pulled away.

"I'm sorry," John tried to explain.

"Don't worry about it." Charlotte was just as much to blame.

She turned and pivoted and walked toward the door. Charlotte got outside and felt a certain tingling sensation and a little light-headed. John was one of the only guys who could make her feel that way. *Oh well,* she thought, *what can I do about that now?*

John sat back down at the table. He had felt it too. There was the chemistry, electricity, spark, and connection—whatever you want to call it? It was definitely there. She knew it and more importantly he knew it. And he knew his life would become even more complicated than it already was.

He had come to Provo on blind faith that the one girl who he'd never let escape his brain would still have feelings for him. Whether or not the feelings were strong enough to endure he was not sure, but now he knew she had thought about him. And then John stopped: *What are you doing? She's engaged. You saw the rock. She's taken, and will be for all time and eternity. Get this out of your head, John. It's done. The game is over.*

But then another side of his brain kicked in. *And what if she's not totally happy and she's settling with this Brian? What if I was the 'What If' guy she's always had in the back of her mind? And now I'm here in front of her making a play on her affections.* Then the other side kicked back in. *Yeah. But you can't make a play for her affections. You can't see her, touch her, talk to her, and breathe her in, because she's with somebody else whom she's made a commitment to.* John had this civil war within his brain for about fifteen minutes.

Finally, Kurt interrupted John. "Dude, you have to leave. I need this table."

He stood up, smiled and squeezed Kurt's shoulder, "She still likes me, Kurt. And I have nothing to lose."

Kurt smiled politely.

"Right on, Man."

CHAPTER 9

John's flight home to L.A. was quick and painless. The whole time he wrote on a yellow legal notepad about what he needed to do. He had to devise a strategy so complex and detailed to be able to shadow Charlotte and then spend time with her behind Brian's back. John had decided he didn't like the name Brian. His thoughts lingered. *And who is this Brian guy anyway? Is he as cool as me? I don't think so.*

Charlotte still liked him and John had to do something drastic so he decided to take a risk.

His brother-in-law Matt told him wisely one day, "If you want to own your destiny, you must take a risk, but it must be a calculated risk."

John wasn't sure if his risk was calculated. Sometimes he thought maybe it could be considered calculated by a madman. But all of that didn't matter. John's mind was made up. He was going to move to Provo and pursue Charlotte.

The smile on John's face was bigger than the Joker from the Batman movie as he walked into his boss' office. His boss was Mr. Johnson, a portly man of forty or so with a Zegna dark suit and matching tie. Mr. Johnson had done well for himself in this business.

John sat down but he already knew he'd only need a few minutes.

"John, good to have you back. Glad you're feeling better."

"Thanks. I feel good." John knew he really didn't "feel good" but that was beside the point.

"So, what's up?" Mr. Johnson asked.

John started his pre-planned speech, "I've been working here for almost four years and in that four years I've pretty much done the same kind of boring work day after day. Yes, I was given the viewing pleasure of the glass ceiling and from my view it looks quite nice up there but the truth is, I'm never going to be above the glass ceiling, am I? No, I'm probably not. That set me to thinking about what a good substitute labor force would be for the kind of work I do. Do you know what I came up with. Of course you don't. Well the answer is Monkeys! You would save on your overhead by leaps and bounds if you employed monkeys in the place of people like me."

Mr. Johnson was rubbing his chin.

"Anyway. I've come here today Mr. Johnson to tell you I quit. And I'm sorry I can't give you two weeks notice because I don't have two weeks to give. Today will be my last day here and I wanted to thank you for the opportunity to work with this company, but I must move on. And to sum it all up I think the work I've been doing is 'monkey labor' and that's why I think you should hire monkeys. Why not?"

Mr. Johnson took it all in. John had said more than a mouthful. Mr. Johnson had to try to figure out why he was talking about monkeys—there was something between the lines.

"So, where'd you get a job?" Mr. Johnson ended the silence.

"What?"

"Who poached you away? Come on you can tell me. We're all family here."

"Poached? Look, I'm not going anywhere else."

"John, let's be reasonable. You sound a little disgruntled. What did they offer you?"

"Look. I wasn't offered another job. I'm just sick of working here."

"Let's keep this simple. Just tell me what company gave you

the offer and what they were offering and maybe I can match it. Were they offering stock options?"

Mr. Johnson didn't get it. He could only see what he wanted to see.

"Mr. Johnson, am I talking Chinese or what? There's no other offer. I'm simply cleaning out my desk and walking away. I quit."

"What could I do to make you stay? How about a fifteen thousand bump to your salary?"

John blinked twice at the offer but he had made up his mind. "There's nothing you could do to make me stay."

"Maybe twenty thousand bump and a promise to attach you to our higher profile clients, and to ensure you a steady rise to the executive ranks in about two or three years."

John was considering his next response. *Wow, that was a sizable offer.* "Mr. Johnson. I really have a lot to do today and debating about whether to stay or not is not one of them. I have made up my mind. Thank you again. And good day."

He stood up and walked out the door. He had done it. He had finally done it. Today was the beginning of a new chapter for John Edwards, *Look out world, here I come.*

John rounded his desk. He picked up the box that he had placed all of his personals in. He said his goodbyes to all of his co-workers and headed toward the door to freedom.

Mr. Johnson stood next to his right-hand Man as they both watched John wave at them and then leave the office.

"I want you to find out where he lands. And find out all you can about monkeys and our competitors. I want this to be your top priority." Mr. Johnson leaned over to his right-hand Man.

"Monkeys sir?"

"Did I stutter? Monkeys. Now go."

Mr. Johnson knew something monumental had happened to John. And it had. He was finally right about what he had to do. He had to leave the confines of his nice living, good job, comfortable apartment and go to the cold climate of Provo and chase a girl.

John walked outside and took a couple of deep breaths. He looked up at the fourth floor where his company's offices were and couldn't believe it. Then the practical side of John came out. What are you doing? He offered you a twenty thousand dollar raise and a sure path to becoming an executive. *What were you thinking? Is Charlotte worth all of that? You could find another girl. Maybe you should go back in there and tell Mr. Johnson that you did have another offer and that you have re-considered his offer and would like to stay with the company and would be honored with the salary bump. Think about what you're doing John. Don't be an idiot. This was your big break.* But it was no use. The dreamer, unrealistic, fantasy side of his brain was running the show. And he was in love, or close to it anyway.

CHAPTER 10

Almost eight years earlier John could remember the same scene: saying goodbyes to his friends in California, packing up his car—now a Black Infiniti Q45—and saying goodbye to the sunshine and beaches of Southern California. His Infiniti was a 1994 but he told people it was a 1996. In the end, John didn't care what people thought because the car was all paid for—the only thing he owned.

John headed out on the 101 S. to the 60 E. to the 91 E. to the 15 N. This is how Californians drive, freeway to freeway. John liked the system. It had been a long time since John had driven to Provo but he'd been to Vegas a couple of times in the last year.

In fact, two months prior John had gone to Vegas with one of his buddies. His buddy Paul, likable guy, talked him into going to the Golden Horseshoe in Old Vegas and playing in a twilight game of Texas Hold-Em.

He acquiesced and they found themselves in the back of the casino with a dealer named Larry from Atlanta, Georgia, and a motley crew of professional poker players, truck drivers passing through, and tourists. To the pros John and Paul were tourists, but John and Paul considered themselves skilled players.

Texas Hold-Em was a high stakes game. Lucky for them they were at a 2-6-8 table. The way it was played was quite simple. Each player was given two cards that they could look at no matter what, unless of course somebody bet blind on the flop. Explaining "betting blind" is another matter. Every player would look at the two cards in his own hand and then the dealer would turn over "the flop." The flop was three cards that were held in the middle of the table. All of the players would have to play off them. Now, if somebody thought they had a good hand, they could bet, but the first bet had to be two dollars and so on. Then another player could bet six dollars and then eight and on we go. After the betting of the first go around the dealer would turn over another card and so on until five cards were in the middle. From there players bet on their hand and the one that had the best hand using five cards from the two in their hand and the five in the middle would win. Essentially that was Texas Hold-Em.

John knew he shouldn't have sat down. Gambling was wrong and against the teachings of The Church. Some people need to learn the hard way. In John's life he'd learned a lot of lessons the hard way.

John and Paul had played Texas Hold-Em at home for fun, but this was for real. They were in Vegas playing against guys who did it for a living.

Paul told John one rule before they hit the table. They would both start with $40 and if they lost it they'd walk. It was all for entertainment's sake anyway.

The tourists, John and Paul, sat down next to the pros and truck drivers, pulled out their money and slapped it down. John looked around at the mountains of white chips representing a dollar, red chips representing $25, as well as black chips representing $100. There was a lot of money sitting at the table.

Larry, the dealer cashed in their $40, giving them both a tray of white chips and said, "Good luck."

The game began and unbeknownst to John and Paul the other players were licking their chops. They couldn't wait to take the tourist's money and send them packing. It didn't take long for John and Paul to lose every single one of their chips. John bet the farm on a flush, king high and was shot down by a full house and a sinister smile. Paul was also out and started to stand up. He looked at his watch and couldn't believe it. It only took thirty minutes to lose forty bucks.

Paul knew he was out of his league. "See you guys later. It was fun." None of the other gamblers even acknowledged Paul. They took his money. That's all they wanted from him. John followed Paul but asked Larry to save his seat.

Paul was smiling. "Man, those guys were pros. You see them, just waiting for their cards? And did you see the way their eyes lit up when we sat down?"

John was half-listening but also looking around. He saw an ATM machine and made a bee-line for it.

"Where are you going?" Paul asked and followed.

He put in his ATM card—bad mistake. Never use an ATM machine in a casino. Never. It means you're going to lose that money. And you're going to lose it quick.

Paul tried to stop him. "Dude, they're charging you $2.25 for the transaction."

John was past the point of no return.

"I can beat those guys. I just need a little bit of a bankroll." John had heard that phrase in a movie. John pulled the money out of the ATM.

"How much is that?" Paul asked.

"Three hundred. I can take them." John had already made his decision, usually a good quality but not in that instance.

"Give the money to me. At least you're giving it to somebody you know," Paul pleaded.

"I know what I'm doing Paul. After I'm done with them we'll go to the Rio and have the buffet on me." John patted Paul on the back.

And with that John headed back to the Poker Room.

"I'm not going back in there, man." Paul tried to stop the madness.

"Look Paul. I've never done this before. I make the money, right? So, I should be able to spend it how I want."

Paul started to laugh. "Man. Think about what you're saying. Do you want to give away three hundred bucks, just like that? Those guys know every combination, every angle; basically, they'll use you. Seriously, let's go." Paul tried to be the voice of reason.

John was stubborn. "You know where I'll be."

"You've seen *The Cincinnati Kid* way too many times, man." Paul gave up and threw his hands into the air.

John sat down at the table and pulled out the three hundred and laid it down.

Larry counted it and shouted out, "Changing in three hundred."

John was determined, but it didn't matter. It was a bad mistake, a very bad mistake. It took four hours in all but John lost every penny including an extra two hundred he extracted from the ATM machine at 2 a.m. Five hundred and forty dollars all together was given away that night. He thought his luck had to turn. It had to turn. It never did. And it was an expensive lesson to learn the hard way.

He had just passed the Strip on the I-15. There's no way he'd stop. *No one leaves a winner in Vegas. You will always lose in the end*, he thought.

John had learned his lesson. Never again would he use an ATM machine in a casino and never again would he gamble.

Well, maybe not ever. There was that one time when the California lottery was at ninety-four million. John was at a weak moment, played and of course lost. The only reason he'd played the lotto was that the millions would give him a secure financial foundation. Winning the lotto would give anybody that. John knew he was rationalizing. And rationalization never got you anywhere. Gambling is a "no win."

In learning his lesson the hard way, the five hundred and forty came back to bite him when he needed to pay his bills but couldn't.

He thought about Charlotte as he passed the last of the bright lights of Sin City. *Am I taking a gamble on her? Can it turn? Does she feel the same way about me that I do about her? Is lady luck on my side?*

A risk is a gamble, so anyway he cut it John knew he was taking a gamble going up to Provo.

Chapter 11

"Welcome to St. George." John was two thirds of the way to Provo. In St. George the good radio stations are scarce, especially at 1 a.m. in the morning. John flipped through the stations anyway. He was starting to get tired. He pressed scan and hoped it would land on something good.

A smooth female voice came over the air. "Anybody out there. Here's a goodie from one of my favorite bands, Genesis. Stay awake and be safe."

The piano came in and John was in complete and total disbelief when he started to recognize the song. Was it a sign?

Phil Collins came in belting the refrain leading to the chorus. "Throwing it all away. Throwing it all away. Throwing it all away." John turned off the radio. All of a sudden the quiet was refreshing. He sat in the silence for a moment looking at the dark road ahead. It had all added up and the doubt was back. *Why would that song, out of all of the millions of songs out there be on right now? Coincidence? Destiny?* John wanted to turn around and give up.

He'd hit the wall. The wall where you either push forward hoping for greener pastures or you put your tail between your legs and plead for your former life back. What was he doing? And was it really worth it?

John knew the answers to both of those questions and maybe that's what pushed him forward over the wall. John was doing what he had to for survival and he knew Charlotte was worth it. She was worth all the energy he had in his entire body. That one day John spent with her on the beach was one of the best days of his life. He had realized later, much later, that he was afraid to put himself out there and to stray from "The Plan."

Another best day of his life was when he had lunch with Charlotte in Provo. They talked of old times, and the topper was the hug. He knew she didn't want to let go, and at another time wouldn't have needed to let go. He felt like it was all his fault. Charlotte had been there all along, watching his every move, and waiting for him to notice her.

John was nearing Beaver and his eyes were fading fast. The first snowfall hit Utah early that year and the first week of December received fifty inches. He opened his eyes wide noticing the slick road conditions. He had to stay awake no matter what the cost. John turned the heater on full blast. It worked for a while.

Then he slapped himself lightly on his face. It didn't do much. He tried again, reared back his hand and slapped even harder. "Ow!!!!" The slap stung like no other. That wasn't smart.

John looked out his front windshield and watched the small white flakes land on his car. It was really coming down. *Welcome back to Utah, John.* He pressed his outside temperature control on the dash. Sure enough, it said thirty-one degrees.

It had been a long time since John had driven in snow. He was now past his sleepy state, still tired albeit, but his eyes were aware of the road ahead of him. John kept the speedometer at sixty and his face close to the heater vent.

He never wanted to ask himself that same question again about Charlotte. Was Charlotte worth it? She was worth the sacrifice. The answer was and would always be YES. John decided in his tired, weakened state, that no matter what happened or what he would go through, he wouldn't ever ask that question again as long as he lived.

He kept his steady pace. Out of the blue an eighteen-wheeler, flying faster than any eighteen-wheeler should go, passed right in front of John, sending up a cloud of white. He couldn't see the road, just white. He steered straight and did as he'd been taught as a little kid to do when he was in a precarious or uncertain situation. He said a pleading prayer. Shortly after, the cloud went away and John continued on.

"Not again," John said aloud as another eighteen-wheeler came up fast on his right.

He punched the gas. The speedometer climbed quickly thanks to the super charged V-8 under the hood. The eighteen-wheeler was left in the dust.

John smiled and shook his head. "Not again. Not tonight." John's victory was short-lived as red and blue lights came bearing down on him out of nowhere. His heart sank. *Why today of all days?*

He pulled the Q over to the side of the road. Officer West, young, twenty-eight maybe, with a handle bar moustache, walked up to his window.

"Do you know why I pulled you over?"

That had to be the stupidest question ever invented by man. John thought maybe Cops had to ask that.

"Yes Officer." John had to concentrate. He thought if he was polite and came up with a good story Officer West would let him go. John handed Officer West his driver's license and insurance information.

"I like your mustache." John didn't know why he said that, possibly Officer West was insecure about the mustache and he was padding he ego. He'd try anything.

"Thank you. It'll be a second." Officer West went back to his cruiser.

John wasn't sure how fast he was going. It was all a blur.

Officer West came back to the car. John had heard if you tell a cop a sad story they usually let you off. One of his friends told a cop once that his mother had just died. John couldn't do that. He tried to pull a sad story out of his memory banks, but he was tired, dead tired. There was no inspiration.

If he was a hot girl, all he'd have to do is smile and if that didn't work cry, and as a last resort ask for his phone number. John's older sister Myka was famous for getting out of tickets. Scratch that idea. He wasn't a hot girl. John decided to tell the truth.

He began by telling Officer West that he'd already been passed by an Eighteen-Wheeler and almost crashed because of snow blindness caused by snow thrown on his windshield and he didn't want that to happen again.

"Didn't you see that eighteen-wheeler coming up alongside me?" John begged for mercy.

"All I saw was you, speeding like a screaming banshee."

"Have you ever been in love, Officer West?" John tried to work on Officer West's sensitive side.

"Of course I have."

"Well. I'm driving to Provo to chase a girl. She's everything."

He went on to tell Officer West all about Charlotte and what she was like.

Officer West softened up a little bit. "Look. This is what I'll do. I'll take off the reckless driving. And put you down for only going ten over."

John mumbled under his breath. "That's it?"

"What?" Officer West heard something.

"Thank you."

Officer West handed the ticket over to John.

"How much will this cost me?" John had to think about his finances.

"Probably about fifty."

"Beaver must need a new library." John shouldn't have said that either.

Luckily, Officer West didn't catch the sarcasm. "No. We have a fine library. Oh and good luck with the girl."

"That's what I need." John rolled up his window and pulled away. What a day! John wrote on a piece of paper. "Note to self, never speed through Beaver."

John was finally getting close to Provo and closer to Charlotte. He started to look at the glass half full. The glass half empty he'd drunk already.

CHAPTER 12

Everyone thought the Belmont was the hip place to live in Provo, so John had to get an apartment there. Back when John went to BYU in 1997, the Avenues, or the Enclave or Condo Row were the hip, cool places to live. The Avenues took the prize at that time and was called by most "Melrose Place" after the popular night soap opera created by Aaron Spelling. Of course John lived a semester at Melrose Place. There are three important things to know about Provo—location, location, and location.

The most important reason John wanted to live at the Belmont now was Charlotte. He made sure not to be in the same ward, but he chose an apartment that was only four buildings down from hers.

John was lucky to even get a place. Some guy fried his brain, had a nervous breakdown and moved home. So, a place opened up for him, month to month. Everything was falling into place for John.

His address was 437 N. Belmont Place #160. He grabbed his pillow and blanket out of the unorganized pile of stuff in his car and walked to his apartment. He found his way to his room, dropped on his bed and collapsed into a deep sleep.

The next morning he carried a handful of stuff that included a Fender acoustic guitar to his apartment. John couldn't play a lick but he would learn someday. He walked to his room and set everything down. Last night he didn't have the energy to check everything out. The room was a decent size with a dresser, desk, and a bed for a midget. He knew the bed had to go. His back wouldn't be able to hold up. He'd buy a queen today. A king would make the room too crowded. Other than that he was quite content with his new living arrangement.

He headed back out to his car. That trip he carried in the snowboard, the laptop, and a bag of clothes. It was weird but John felt good, good about every choice he'd made up to that point. He looked out behind him at the majestic mountains covered with snow. It was very peaceful and soothing. He needed some quiet time. John closed his eyes and took in a deep breath of the clean, fresh mountain air.

Charlotte had just finished her last class of the day. It was an Art History elective. Her professor, Dr. Walker, was ancient but had traveled all over the world, taught at Oxford, and had one of his paintings in the Church Office Building in Salt Lake. Dr. Walker had a slight problem. When he talked, spit like drool formed at the corners of his mouth. No matter how much Charlotte tried to ignore it, it still grossed her out. That day was an especially long lecture and Charlotte had to excuse herself to use the bathroom on numerous occasions.

She had two things on her mind. Number one she needed a power nap. Number two she needed to get something to eat.

Her car pulled onto Seven Peaks Boulevard, from 700 south. She decided to take the long way along the whole north side of The Belmont.

John opened his trunk and picked up three black heavy-duty garbage bags, substitute for suitcases. He closed the trunk with his elbow and turned to walk to his apartment.

Charlotte came straight down Belmont Place. John was carrying his things in the distance. He stopped and dropped the black bags on the sidewalk and rushed back to his car. He had forgotten the keys in the trunk lock.

Charlotte's car came towards John as he pulled the keys out of the trunk. Charlotte was a little tired but she noticed a guy standing next to a black car. He looked familiar, she thought. Her cell phone rang as she turned her head to get a second look. It was Brian.

"Hello, honey. Yeah. I'll be home in a little while. I'm starving too." Charlotte hung up the phone, and looked in her rear view mirror but John was gone.

John dumped his black bags on the floor, and started to sort and put away clothes. That's the way guys move. He turned on his laptop, slipped in The Doves and started to organize his world. John knew Charlotte lived down the block in apartment #142. He would have to look for her Land Rover.

Charlotte kicked off her shoes and jumped on her bed. She had a comfortable zebra print comforter on the top, even though she knew the whole zebra and leopard print thing was over. She slept with the zebra comforter every night because she made it. In fact, Charlotte made the pillows, comforter, and pillowcases on her bed. She was a gifted seamstress and created many of the designs that she used. She had considered moving to Paris and going to one of the world's greatest art schools. However, she knew she wanted to be a mom more than anything.

Charlotte's roommates were all smart, independent, hot, and pursued by a majority of the male student body at BYU. Charlotte and her roommates always talked about what it would be like to marry someone you were truly, madly in love with.

They would sit there for hours and talk about names they'd thought of for their unborn children. Sure the girls liked to party and have fun but more than anything they wanted to fall in love and get married.

She set her alarm on her cell phone as her eyes started to

fade. Forty-five minutes was all she needed. Her body was exhausted and before she knew it, she was sleeping. She looked peaceful, like an angel.

If any girl ever had "the glow," it was her. "The Glow" was a phrase John and his buddies always talked about. Good people, beautiful people, genuine people, seem to have a special "glow" or "light" coming from them. John knew the scriptures said it was a "light of righteousness." John and his buddies used to look at girls and notice which ones did and didn't have "the glow."

During his time in L.A. he'd met a couple of non-Mormon girls with "the glow," but it was rare. Every time he looked at Charlotte he saw that light, "the glow."

Charlotte turned over but she was definitely asleep. Her face was soft and her eyes were moving a little. Her hand came down to her left. She was dreaming.

She found herself standing on a vibrant green meadow of grass. The grass went on forever every which way. She looked up at the sky, bluer than any day she'd seen before. Charlotte bent down and touched the grass. It was real, soft and wavy.

A figure walked toward her from the distance of a good football field away. She could tell it was a man. She stood up and started to walk toward him. The pace quickened, as the man walked faster toward her. She stopped immediately when she could make out the man's face.

The man kept walking, stopped inches from her, and then walked around her. Charlotte closed her eyes and stood still. The man ran his hand across her back and up to her hair. He tenderly grabbed a handful of her hair, and pulled her head back.

She opened her eyes to see the man's face again. It was John, those eyes, and soft lips. She melted in his arms and their lips came together. The entire sky became a piercing white light as they lifted up into the air toward it.

"I'm here. Don't worry." John held her tight and she felt safe.

Brian had already entered Charlotte's room. He was watching her sleep. He'd been there for sometime and didn't want to disturb her.

Charlotte lifted up her head and opened her eyes.

"You're so peaceful when you sleep." Brian looked down at her.

Charlotte was out of breath. She couldn't speak right away.

"Are you okay?" Brian was concerned.

"Yes. I was dreaming." Charlotte took a deep breath. *What are you doing here?*

Brian anxiously asked, "What was it about?"

The dream was still in her head. She'd awakened with the memory intact.

"It's all fuzzy." She wanted to end the conversation.

"Was I in it?" Brian wanted something more.

"Of course you were in it. You ran to me in a vacant green meadow and grabbed me and kissed me." Charlotte hoped that would satisfy him.

She couldn't tell him she dreamed about John. Nor could she tell Brian about all of the dreams she'd had of John in the past.

"Really. How did I grab you?" Brian thought he was the man. If he only knew the truth, it would crush his male ego moment.

"You grabbed me like this." She grabbed Brian and planted a wet one on him. Charlotte was always the aggressor. Brian was passionate, just a little lackadaisical.

"I wish I had dreams like that." Brian was milking it for everything he could.

Charlotte would remember that dream for a long time.

She'd remember that John ran towards her in that surreal field and kissed her. What did it mean? She probably didn't want to know.

CHAPTER 13

John had a bit of a dilemma. He was still paying for his condo in Los Angeles, credit card bills, and now his place at The Belmont. He had enough cash for a couple of weeks but it would dwindle in no time. The solution. He needed a job.

He searched everywhere. Novell, Micron, even tried to get a job doing the dreaded multi-level marketing for Nu-Skin and Noni. Nothing. Absolutely nothing. The economy in Provo had hit an all-time low; no one was hiring—even the church put a freeze on hiring people. John looked at his options. He could budget his money or swallow his pride and take whatever jobs were out there.

He drove down Main Street in downtown Provo. He passed Buona Vita, the new Italian restaurant where he'd met Charlotte a week earlier. He parked his car and walked in the front door.

The same hostess was at the front and she remembered him. "Let me guess. You want that table over there and Kurt to wait on you."

"Actually, is your manager here?" John asked with a smile. He had to be nice.

"Stay right here. I'll get Will."

Will Nathanson, thirties, handsome guy with tired eyes, walked up to John. "Can I help you?"

John turned around, a familiar voice. "Will. What's up man? It's John. You remember me?"

Will grabbed John's hand and they patted each other's back—the way guys hug.

"So, what are you doing here?" Will wanted to hear every-thing.

"In Provo? Just hanging out. You look good, man. So, this is your place?"

"Yeah. I opened it about six months ago with a friend of mine. I'm the owner, manager, executive chef, host, and dish-washer, whatever you need. How did you know I was here?"

"I didn't know. I'm kind of looking for a job. I ate here last week, liked the food and said why not." John was being completely honest.

"You sure you want to wait tables."

"I'll wash dishes if that's all you have available."

"Can you start tomorrow?"

"When?" John let out a sigh of relief. He'd have some money coming in.

"How about noon? That's when the training will begin."

"Sounds good. Thanks again, man. I owe you."

"Don't worry about it." Will headed back to the kitchen. He was the glue that held the restaurant together.

John went outside into the cold air but felt extremely warm, toasty and happy inside. It was all working out. At least financially he'd be able to survive whatever happened to him, unless he got fired.

Why did he say that? John needed good thoughts, happy thoughts from here on out. He walked down Center Street and it was cold again. He remembered why he liked living in Southern Cal. Oh well, he was there for a reason. And what a beautiful reason she was.

Charlotte was still feeling a little guilty about the dream. She couldn't get it out of her head. Why had she dreamt about John? Why couldn't it have been Brian? Well, first off, Brian would never grab her that way, the aggression, the passion. That wasn't his style.

The first time Charlotte and Brian really kissed was on their sixth date. She wondered if he was ever going to kiss her at all. Brian had taken her to see a play at the HFAC. It was about Mormon Pioneer women. Charlotte liked the play but would've rather gone dancing, horseback riding, or rock climbing. They always went to plays.

Charlotte started to tickle Brian's neck during the Second Act. He told her people could see them. She thought that was the point. The play went on for three hours and Charlotte had to basically fold her arms the whole time. The curtain finally came down and she hurried out the door. She needed some fresh air quick.

There was two feet of newly fallen snow. Charlotte ran over to the snow like a little kid. "Let's make snow angels."

"You've got to be kidding, Charlotte. It must be thirty degrees out here. You'll freeze."

"Come on Brian. Make a snow angel with me." She gave him that sultry, "just do it" look.

Brian shook off the look. "I'm thinking for both of us. Do you want to catch a cold?"

He was the king of reason. Who would want to have a cold?

Charlotte knew, however, there was something beautiful about a spontaneous action.

"Sometimes you get a cold, Brian. Sometimes the cold gets you." Charlotte looked up into the sky as she dropped back into a mound of snow. As soon as she hit, her arms moved up and down like wings. She rolled over to look at her creation. "The first snow angel of our first winter together." Charlotte was proud of her spontaneous act. She brushed off the snow and ran over to Brian. She gave him a big hug, getting the rest of the snow all over him.

"You're such a wild one. And that's why I like you so much. Let's go get you warm." Brian wrapped his arms around her and they walked to the car.

The whole way home Brian kept talking about how crazy it was for Charlotte to make that snow angel in the thirty-degree weather. It must've been fascinating conversation for him because he wouldn't let it go.

Charlotte just smiled. That was Brian. He was polite, respectful, reserved, and considerate and often boring.

Brian walked Charlotte to her door.

"Charlotte, I had a great time tonight, as I always do with you. I still can't believe you did that snow angel."

Most of the girls Brian dated must've had the personality of a wet sponge.

"Yeah. It was crazy," she said.

"And that's what I like about you Charlotte. You are yourself."

"Well, thank you Brian."

"And Charlotte. I've been wanting to ask you this question for a long time." Brian moved closer to her. She was waiting.

"Go ahead."

"Can I kiss you?" Brian was relieved to finally get it off his chest.

Charlotte did a double take in her head. Like most women Charlotte enjoyed the anticipation, the waiting, and then bam, here come his lips. That's how the first kiss should happen. It should be consensual and out of the blue.

One time during Charlotte's freshman year at BYU she went out with another nice guy. They had a decent time on the date and then the nice guy asked her if he could kiss her. Charlotte started laughing and couldn't stop. The nice guy walked away, crushed ego and all, alone into the sunset.

Was it polite for the guy to ask if he could kiss you? Sure. But that wasn't what Charlotte wanted. She wanted to be taken by surprise, build the suspense, and then the fireworks.

Charlotte knew it was coming that night. Brian was especially nervous. She decided if he asked she wouldn't laugh at him.

She looked into his eyes and smiled. "Yes. You may kiss me."

Brian moved in slowly and steady like. His lips pressed against hers and Charlotte waited for the rocket launch, fireworks, flash of light, tingles all over her body, or anything at all.

"Have a great night." Brian moved away. It was over.

The first kiss was in the history books. Obviously Brian was floored by the kiss. He was smiling from ear to ear.

Charlotte opened the door to her apartment and walked in. She dropped her purse to the ground and touched her lips. Why didn't she feel anything? She liked Brian. Maybe it would take some time.

Her roommate, Rachel, 5'9", drop dead body, and long blond hair walked in right after Charlotte.

"What's the matter?" Rachel was prying.

"Brian just kissed me."

"And how was it?" Rachel wanted all of the dirt.

"It was . . . it was great," Charlotte lied.

"So, the nice guy has nice lips."

"How was your date?" Charlotte wanted to change the subject.

"I didn't really like him. He drove an old Toyota Camry. Goodnight honey." Rachel went to her room.

Charlotte knew her first kiss with Brian wasn't great but she liked him all the same. As time went on the kisses got better, still forced at times, but thanks to her nonchalant tutorials, there was progress.

Charlotte almost went through a red light. She looked up just in time and slammed on her brakes. She knew Brian wasn't passionate like John, but he brought other qualities to the table that John didn't have. She told herself it was a trade off. Charlotte was going to marry Brian in four months, so no more thinking about John, and especially no more dreams about John.

CHAPTER 14

Sundays are always busy days in Provo, especially near BYU with the horde of singles going to their prospective sacrament meetings. The last time John went to a sacrament meeting in Provo was on Fast and Testimony Sunday. Some testimonies were sweet and tender, others were travelogues, and then what would a BYU Fast and Testimony Meeting be like without a girl or two getting up and saying how much they loved their roommates. Sometimes John wished there was a lesson once a month on how you should bear your testimony. He liked to hear the testimonies of recent converts. They were simple, to the point, with no fat, and brought an abundance of the Spirit.

John was born in the church but he had great respect for converts. His dad was a convert.

His mom wrote his dad a forty page "Dear John" telling him why she couldn't marry him. She could have summed it up in one sentence. You are not Mormon. His dad read the "Dear John" three times and then went to find the Mormon Church near the Air Force base he was stationed at in Montana. He found the church, embraced it, was baptized, called John's mom and, like they say, the rest was history.

Converts were amazing to John. They gave up everything; their friends and families disowned them in many cases, but it only made them stronger and with greater conviction.

He wanted to believe with the same power converts had. Since his mission John had struggled to keep the same level of spirituality. In his work setting, he was bombarded with profanity, lewd jokes, and the use of the Lord's name in vain. The last one was the one that bugged him the most. It would send a chill down his spine whenever someone in the office used the Lord's name in vain.

John knew he was blessed to have been raised by righteous and loving parents, who lived the gospel by word and deed. It seemed the older he got the more he struggled with some things. He understood why the leaders of the church tell the newly returned missionaries to get married. John knew he could never completely progress spiritually without a wife. Sometimes he felt like his spiritual progress was stagnant.

He was a twenty-seven-year-old virgin but he'd made some mistakes with one of his girlfriends. It was late one night and they were just cuddling. One thing led to another as it grew late, and John began to touch her where his hands shouldn't go. He knew it was a mistake before he did it, but somehow he was able to convince himself that everything would be okay. And it felt good at the time.

The next morning it wasn't okay. He felt awful and ashamed as well. It had been a couple of years and he had confessed it to his bishop but John was hard on himself. He knew the temptation was always there. John was grateful to have a conscience and more importantly a testimony of the gospel and its teachings.

Over the years John had met randomly with people he'd known from his BYU days. Many of them were married; others were traveling down different paths. They had let go of the iron rod. And it was the same story—it never happened over night. It happened little by little, one sin at a time.

John met Carl Saunders in New York on a business trip. They were both on the subway going to downtown Manhattan. Carl looked familiar to John but he didn't know why. He looked at him again and this time Carl caught him looking his way.

"Do I know you?"

"I don't know. What's your name?"

"I don't know. What's your name?" Carl was messing with John a little.

"John Edwards."

"It does sound familiar." Carl was searching his brain.

"Did you go to BYU?"

"Man, what a small world. What are you doing here, John?" It finally dawned on Carl.

"You remember me, then?"

"Yeah. We were in the same ward at The Avenues."

John remembered Carl well. Carl was from Northern Cal, went to BYU on a full-ride scholarship, and could have gone anywhere. He turned down Harvard and Stanford. He was intelligent, traveled the world, had his own opinion, and treated everyone with the same respect and courtesy. John always knew Carl would become something great. He had that intangible thing about him.

"So, do you live in New York?"

"Manhattan," Carl corrected him.

"What are you up to?" John was sincerely interested. He'd often thought about what happened to Carl Saunders.

"Not much. I worked on Wall Street for a couple of years and now I have my own shop and manage rich people's money."

"Sounds like a good operation." John knew nothing about Wall Street.

"It pays the bills. Keeps me busy. What are you doing now, John?"

"I work for a computer company in L.A. Nothing important. Hey, I'm glad I ran into you. I'll be here on Sunday as well. Do you know where the best singles ward meets?" John hoped it was near his hotel.

"Wouldn't know," Carl said in a short tone.

"Are you married?"

"Don't have time for that. No. I don't really go to church anymore." Carl wasn't shy about telling everything, never was.

Right there John's mouth almost dropped to the ground. At BYU, John had always seen Carl at church, giving talks, and participating in lessons.

"When did that happen?" John knew that came out wrong.

"Church?"

John shook his head.

"I think I went to church because everyone else was going to church. It was the social thing to do. I don't think I ever believed."

John hoped there'd never be the day when he'd echo those same words. John believed. He believed it all. He believed in Christ and the atonement. He believed in the Plan of Salvation, the war in heaven, and the time of probation to choose good from evil. John believed in the restoration of the gospel, and the translation of the Book of Mormon by Joseph Smith. And he believed President Gordon B. Hinckley was the mouthpiece for the Lord on the earth.

He believed Heavenly Father answered his prayers. And he knew the church was true. John felt it, from the top of his head to the bottom of his toes, taking a line from his Dad. He'd felt peace, beauty, calm, and above all, love. These feelings confirmed to him that it was true. He had too many experiences to confirm his belief and he could never deny the truth of the gospel, never could, no matter how hard he'd tried over the years.

John sat there, back in Provo, at the fast and testimony meeting as his thoughts raced in his head and heart. Some of the testimonies really touched him. He liked sitting in church and listening. There was a power there.

After Sacrament Meeting there was always fifteen to thirty minutes of dead time. In Mormon terminology at BYU, dead time meant social time. Time to mingle and talk amongst yourselves. It's truly an amazing sight to see over two hundred singles bounce around talking to friends, unknowns, or simply people they're attracted to and want to get to know better. John was no stranger to the social ways of Provo. He saw some people who looked familiar and decided to make his way over to them.

Every conversation began similarly, "Dude, do I know you?"

John had forgotten how small the Mormon single world was. He soon realized he knew more than half of the crowd of guys and girls. In fact, he'd dated some of the girls or their roommates in the past. A lot of girls were new faces, something that was simply wonderful about Provo.

Most of the guys were in their late-twenties to early thirties. Some of them had classes with John during his BYU days, while others dated the same girls, or he just knew their faces from the whole party scene. John couldn't believe it. Some of the guys he had known from the past had come back to Provo from all over; including Huntington Beach, New York, Mesa, Chicago, San Francisco, L.A., and even from overseas. Provo was the Mecca for Mormon singles. Most of the guys had never left Provo. They had just bought condos, found decent jobs, and stayed around the social scene.

One of John's friends was Alex. Alex was thirty-two and twice he'd been engaged and called it off. He drove a silver Yukon Denali. That was a popular car of the single and over-thirty crowd in Provo.

"So, what are you still doing here?" John talked sometimes

before thinking.

"I haven't been here the whole time. I came back in 1999. Besides, look around, I keep getting older and the girls keep getting younger." Alex smiled and at the same time checked out a hot twenty-year-old brunette.

John let that sink in. It was true. Most of these guys told him about the twenty-year-olds they were dating and how hot they were. It was commonplace to let the other guys know that you're dating a hot chick. Then guys give the thumbs up.

The simple reason is guys are insecure. If your bros give the "right on" to a particular girl then the guy is more confident about hanging out with her. John knew it was ridiculous the way it worked.

The chatter toned down as the "dead time" ended. Now it was time to go to Sunday School classes. A tall blonde, maybe 5'7" walked by John so he'd take notice.

"Who is that?" He realized he'd said it out loud. She definitely heard it. She turned around slowly and smiled, disappearing into a gospel doctrine class.

There lay the one problem with Provo. And possibly it was the reason why there were so many attractive, talented, and successful singles in Provo. Everywhere you looked there was someone new you'd like to date. It was almost as if heads were on a swivel, waiting for something better.

John thought about the tall blonde but then his mind turned to Charlotte. He decided he wouldn't try to date anyone, no matter how hot, how smart, or how cool the girl was. His time there would be dedicated to Charlotte.

He knew Charlotte's ward started an hour later than his, thus, he could wait a little longer to get a glimpse of her. John knew she'd be on Brian's arm but that didn't bother him. He simply had to see the reason he threw his plan out the window, quit his job, and drop kicked his future into space. John really didn't want to have any interaction with Charlotte, not just yet. He only wanted to see her angelic face and witness her timeless smile from afar.

John decided it was best to hang outside the Pardoe Theater and wait. Guys and girls passed, picking up programs on their way and headed into the Pardoe. He knew he wouldn't have to wait long. Charlotte was always on time.

She rounded the corner. She had on a tan suede skirt with the hemline at her knees with black boots and a black Prada top. John looked long enough to get a good look. She floored him every single time he laid eyes on her. There she was. She was worth it. She was even worth the speeding ticket on the way over. She was worth everything. She was worth everything he'd given away or better yet thrown away. Even for the chance to be with Charlotte for a moment, he'd do it all over again. And as expected, grinning from car to car was Brian in a Brooks Brother suit. Brian knew he had scored. It was obvious.

John was satisfied. He knew there'd be another time and disappeared into the gospel doctrine class.

Chapter 15

What would Steve McQueen do? John had watched *The Getaway* with McQueen and the beautiful Ali McGraw the night before. Steve McQueen was the definition of cool. John had to be like him. He had to be cool, calculated, and take his time. John could do that, no problem.

He had always been pretty cool, not as cool as McQueen, but he had been cool enough. John thought about his other favorite Steve McQueen movie. It was called *Bullitt*. In *Bullitt* everything was coming down around McQueen's character but he took it in stride. He kept the girl, caught the bad guy, and saved the day.

That was exactly what John wanted to do. He wanted to win the girl, and save the day. Brian could find someone else. John had to have Charlotte. He couldn't go on without her. Now John was getting somewhere. Steve McQueen wouldn't let the girl slip through his fingers. There was no way John could either.

John knew Charlotte's last class on Monday was at 3 p.m. He wasn't stalking her or anything—he'd just done his homework. He looked down at his watch.

"Here she comes." He went into a slow jog heading by the north parking lot at BYU.

Charlotte pulled out her keys and opened the door to her Land Rover. John jogged right in front of her car. She looked up and saw him. Then he saw her.

"Charlotte?" John knew exactly what he was doing. Steve McQueen would've been proud of the smooth, cool approach.

She got out of the car and walked over to John with a surprised smile.

"What are you doing here?"

"I'm just getting some exercise." He had to play coy.

"No. Not that. In Provo. What are you doing in Provo, again?"

"I moved here last week. I got this great job. Couldn't pass it up." Pinocchio couldn't have said it better.

"Oh, that's great. So, you're living here. Where?"

"The Belmont." He knew she had to be aware that he was just down the way from her.

"The Belmont. That's where I live."

"No way. That's crazy. I heard it's really cool." John remained constant, never expressing any emotion.

"Yeah. The Belmont is cool. What apartment?" she asked.

"In 160. What about you?"

"I live in 142. You're in 160? You're just a couple of buildings down from me." Charlotte didn't need to know that.

"Well, I better get going. I have a couple miles to get under my belt." John turned to leave.

"All right. I'll see you around," Charlotte said, dumbfounded.

"Take care." He jogged away, leaving Charlotte with her thoughts.

John kept jogging until he was out of Charlotte's sight. Then he stopped and walked to his car. He didn't really like to jog. It made him look skinny like a rock star. He preferred to swim laps or run hills.

The encounter went well. Now Charlotte knew John was back in town and back into her thoughts.

When it came down to it, Steve McQueen might have done it differently. McQueen probably would've pulled up on his Harley, grabbed Charlotte, driven away, and never turned back. John didn't have a Harley but the thought of doing that did cross his mind.

He was thankful Brian wasn't like Steve McQueen. John knew he wouldn't have a chance if Steve McQueen was with Charlotte.

Life was good for John. He could tell Charlotte was torn between being happy and completely stunned. John had a good laugh. He'd never seen her that way before. She was such a complex and beautiful person. He had made the first move.

CHAPTER 16

Charlotte drove fast to her apartment. She had to tell someone, anyone. Okay, not anyone—Brian would freak. She had held it all in for so long.

Her car flew through the streets surpassing every posted speed limit sign.

She pulled into her parking spot, leaving her car in a weird diagonal. She didn't care. She rushed to the apartment. She had too much going on in her life.

"Anybody home? Anybody?"

Charlotte went straight back to her roommates' bedrooms. Michelle, her roommate from Texas was probably still in class. So she proceeded to Rachel's room.

Rachel had on headphones, singing out loud to *Radiohead*, and was painting her nails. Charlotte stood right in front of her. Rachel didn't budge. She must've had the volume at the maximum decibels.

Charlotte couldn't wait any longer. She was going to explode. Slowly she removed the headphones from Rachel's head.

"Hey Charlotte," Rachel said, finally paying attention.

"Do you have a moment?" Charlotte knew she was reaching the breaking point.

"Sure. What's up?"

Charlotte began at the beginning. The very first time she met John at EFY with Hope and how she'd had a big crush on him. How she'd written him on his mission, and then she slowed down to tell Rachel about their first and only kiss on the beach.

Next Rachel was brought up to speed about seeing John at the Buona Vita restaurant, and how she had just bumped into him at BYU today and on top of it all that she was getting married to Brian in four months.

"I don't need this right now." Charlotte dropped back on Rachel's bed.

"It'll be okay, hon," Rachel tried to console her while blowing on her wet nails.

"Do you think this was all a coincidence, or what?" Charlotte needed answers.

"I don't know Charlotte. Did John know you were already engaged?"

"He said he didn't. And sounded surprised when I told him. He said he was just in town and wanted to catch up. I'm so confused. John complicates everything. I should have never met him at the restaurant." Charlotte put her hands to her head.

"Why? Why does he complicate everything?" Rachel put her hand on Charlotte's back.

"I had a dream the other day and John was in it. The whole dream was about him. He ran to me and then grabbed me passionately and kissed me."

"Oh no." Rachel was starting to see the problem.

"Yeah."

"Do you have feelings for John?" Rachel knew it was getting good.

"I don't know. Yes. Yes, I do. But they're suppressed feelings. I can't let them out." Charlotte started to shed some tears.

"Hey. What's the matter?" Rachel put her arm around Charlotte.

"I'm a horrible person. I'm cheating on Brian and I'm not even married to him yet." Charlotte couldn't help herself and Rachel lent a shoulder.

"You're not cheating on him. You haven't done anything wrong. You didn't plan this."

"You're right. I didn't plan this." Charlotte lifted up her head and wiped the tears away.

"You love Brian, right?"

Charlotte shook her head. Yes.

"And this John guy, is he a great guy like Brian?"

"They're a little different." Charlotte smiled.

"How are they different?" Rachel had never had the opportunity to have Charlotte spill her guts. She was enjoying herself.

"Well, John is really handsome, and has piercing blue eyes, he's funny, sexy, and always says the right thing. He's got great style and a strong yet mischievous smile, and great abs. There's just something about John."

"Man. You have been thinking about him. He sounds perfect." The whole description of John intrigued Rachel. Maybe she needed to find out who he was.

"Brian does have some qualities John doesn't have." Charlotte tried to give Brian some props.

"Is Brian better-looking than John?"

"They have different looks. John is a little more rugged."

Rachel continued the comparison. "Is Brian smarter than John?"

"Brian is really smart but John is a really intelligent guy too." Charlotte knew Rachel wouldn't find out anything with the questioning.

"I got it. Who has better lips? Is Brian a better kisser?" Rachel was waiting to hear that one.

"Thanks for everything," Charlotte said and stood up to leave.

"Come on. You have to tell me." Rachel started to laugh.

"Ha, ha. Fine. They're both good kissers. Do we have any ice cream?" Charlotte tried to hide the lie.

"I don't think so. Do you want me to go get some?"

"No. It's probably better that we don't. I'll eat the whole tub."

"Do you know what's important, honey? To be with someone that makes you happy. That's all that matters." Rachel always ended conversations with a strong, poignant last thought.

She put on her headphones and started to sing out loud.

Charlotte went into her room and fell onto her bed. That's all she ever wanted. She wanted to be happy. Charlotte wanted to marry someone that would make her happy.

Brian made her happy. He did everything to make her feel good about herself. Constantly, he showered her with compliments and words of encouragement and when he held her she felt good.

Charlotte was not the type that liked drama. In fact, she tried to avoid it at all costs. If she wanted drama she'd watch a Spanish soap opera. Not that she'd understand anything.

Now her life was just that—DRAMA.

She had a little headache, her brain was on overdrive, and her heart was confused for the first time since she had said, "Yes, I'll marry you Brian."

Charlotte took two Advil and downed it with water. She lay back in her bed with her thoughts and stared at the ceiling. Maybe that will take care of the headache. What would she do for her heart?

CHAPTER 17

It had been five years since John had waited tables. He'd waited tables everywhere in Utah including: Chili's, Outback Steakhouse, Carver's, Bennett's Bar' B' Que and Grill (The Chuckwagon was the best platter), the Garden Wall Restaurant at Thanksgiving Point, and lastly the Macaroni Grill in Huntington Beach after he graduated from BYU. He knew what was expected of him.

John had on a clean white shirt, black pants, and a smile. His first guests were a newly married student couple. He knew that right off the bat when they ordered water and didn't want to look at the appetizers. He also knew he was going to get a small tip too, regardless whether he gave them the best service possible or not.

The couple looked so young.

"If you don't mind me asking, how old are you guys?" John had to know.

"I'm Mark, just turned twenty-two and my wife is nineteen." He must've been asked that a lot.

John got sat again with another couple in his section. He had to hurry and get Mark and Melanie their water and then greet the new couple.

He dropped off the water in no time and got the drink orders from the new table.

He could do this job, no sweat. It was just like riding a bike. Once you serve you can always go back. John continued to receive more tables but he was on top of it. Every one of his tables was taken care of, and more importantly they were all happy.

John looked at Mark and Melanie. He couldn't believe they were married. They looked like they were still in high school. John knew there was no way he looked like Mark when he was twenty-two. They were kids. What were they doing married? It boggled John's mind.

He spilled some pesto sauce on his shirt delivering a dish to one of his tables.

"Great." John tried to wipe off the green gook. It was no use. He threw the paper towel in the trash and headed back out to his tables with a smile, maybe a fake one.

"Everything all right here?" John asked every table, including Mark and Melanie's. He knew just how to deal with guests.

Will walked up behind John. "How's everything?"

"Couldn't be better." John was in a rhythm.

"You know it's my job to check on you, right? Even though we're friends, nothing is different."

"Right on man." He thought Will was acting a little strange. Will must be stressed out, too many long hours, and not enough down time.

Will disappeared into the kitchen. John's tables still looked content.

John looked over at Mark and Melanie. Melanie was only NINETEEN! There were days when John had wished he'd bit the bullet and just gotten married young.

He always heard those great stories from older couples reminiscing about their poor student days when all they had was each other.

John thought about what it would've been like to go to BYU married. How weird would that have been? Maybe he wouldn't have had as much fun as he did.

When he was on his mission, he'd thought of coming home and then making the leap of faith and getting married. There was always the question that lingered—to whom?

It just wasn't part of "The Plan." John wasn't sure if "The Plan" had done anything for him at all. "The Plan" helped him focus but it also kept him from venturing out and opening himself up to fall in love. He didn't go to BYU to fall in love. He went to BYU to get his degree with honors, have fun, date a lot of girls, and then get into his career. After all of that he could fall in love.

John watched Mark feed Melanie. He was gentle and took his time.

He became lost in his thoughts. Maybe those two are in love as much as anyone else in the world. And if you're in love, the next step is marriage. So what if they struggle, live in a tiny apartment, and usually eat Top Ramen for dinner every night. They have each other and that's all you need to survive. Maybe John was wrong. He should've been looking for love right off his mission. He was just scared. He was scared of the commitment, responsibility, and the other mouth to feed. Those two kids are probably the luckiest two people in the world.

"Waiter. Waiter." It was almost heard throughout the entire restaurant. It was Mark. He was snapping his fingers.

John came out of the trance and went to their table.

"Yes. Do you need anything else?"

"The check. We've been waiting forever." All of the sudden, the nice, sweet, young Mark became a real human being.

"Sorry about that. I thought you weren't done yet." He tried to smooth things over.

"I haven't touched the plate for at least fifteen minutes." Mark wanted to debate it for some reason.

"No problem. Do you want to pay with cash or credit card?"

Mark slid an AMEX card over to John.

"I'll be right back. Sorry for the delay." John hurried over to the Micros machine. He looked at the credit card. It had the name of Samuel McMorrow on it. John knew the kid's name was Mark. That's weird.

Will was standing behind John again.

"Stop doing that. You're creeping me out." John was serious. What was his deal?

"Is everything okay with that table? I heard he was screaming for you."

"He wasn't screaming. Aren't we overdoing this a little?"

"Whatever John. He snapped his fingers for you."

"Something like that." John just wanted the night to be over with.

"You sure you're okay?" Will had to make sure.

"I'm sure. Dude, it's just crazy. I've never had someone snap their fingers at me." John wanted some sympathy.

"Make him happy. Tell him we'll comp him a dessert." And with that Will disappeared again.

John walked over to Mark and Melanie's table. "Hey Mark. This card says Samuel McMorrow."

"I know. It's my father. It's my card. He just pays for it. Here. This is a legal document."

Mark handed John a notary certified document that entitled Mark McMorrow the right to sign his name on his dad's card. Now John had seen it all.

"See. His signature is right there."

"Huh. I've never seen this before."

"It's all legit. Can you please hurry up? We're going to be late for our movie." Mark looked at Melanie and shook his head.

"I'll be right back."

John hurried back over to the Micros machine and ran the card.

He placed the card and credit card slip in front of Mark with some mints. Mark signed it quickly. He put his coat on, helped Melanie with hers and then left.

Maybe John was completely wrong. Most of these young couples have money backing them.

John went to clear the table. Mark and Melanie left a mess. He picked up the credit card slip. He didn't like to look at the tip amount until the end of the night. He couldn't resist looking at that one.

One dollar. They had left him a single dollar on a bill of over fifty dollars. John could understand if they were poor students like his sister Hope, but they weren't. They were spoiled rich kids who got married knowing they had a bank for support. It made him sick how he had thought they were so nice, cute, and innocent. And how long did he make them wait? Fifteen minutes maybe—it was more like ten minutes. John knew he was bitter.

He stuffed the credit card slip into his apron. He was poor. He'd never had his mom or dad backing him financially in his life. They gave him moral support and life advice but that was it.

The rest of the night went well but now John was suspicious anytime he saw a young married couple in his section. Maybe they were all trust fund babies. That's why they got married so young. He wasn't sure if any of his thoughts were making any sense.

He didn't care. He was still a little peeved about the treatment he received from Mark and Melanie. If John had loaded parents, maybe he would've got married young.

It was kind of like being a trapeze artist. They are willing to do death-defying stunts high up in the air because they know there's a safety net to catch them if they fall. John never had a safety net. And if getting married was like doing a trapeze stunt then he needed the safety net. And "The Plan" was his safety net and the answer for everything. Except "The Plan" failed and John had to improvise.

Will was saying goodbye to the last customers of the night.

John had forgotten how exhausting it was to serve. His back was killing him and his feet were on fire. He looked down at his shirt and smiled. It was covered with sauces and butter. It looked like an abstract painting by Pollock or Basquiat. John laughed again. Laughter was the only thing that would make him feel better.

Will walked over to John and patted him on the back. "What a long night. How do you feel?"

"I feel good, I guess. My feet are a little sore." John wanted to talk about something else.

"And how were the customers? Any complaints?"

"Please don't talk to me like that." John couldn't take it anymore.

"Like what?" Will was missing the boat, big time.

"Like you don't know me. I get the feeling that you think you can't treat me any different than the other servers, but there's no one here but me, so, drop it." John put his arms out. The restaurant was empty.

"It's not me, man. It's this place, the job. I never thought owning a restaurant would be so much work."

"I understand bro. You've got a lot on your plate." John patted Will on the back.

"Sometimes I think my head is going to explode. You know, just shoot right off my neck."

"Maybe you need a vacation." John wanted to provide the answer to put Will at ease.

"I mean, everybody's calling, everybody needs me. And my girlfriend wants to date other guys," Will added.

"Sorry to hear that man."

"She says I'm never around. Well, I don't get out of here until ten or eleven every night. And then I go to her place but I usually fall asleep." Will wanted to bear his soul.

"And she's upset that you always fall asleep and never talk to her." John knew the routine.

"Exactly."

"I've been in one of those situations bro. You need someone else here to take some stress off you."

John was always great for having answers for other people, just not himself.

"How about you?" Will just wanted to hear a simple yes.

"Me. No. I have no experience. You don't want me to be a manager."

"Why not? You know everything about a restaurant. You've worked in enough anyway. And the things you don't know I'll teach you." Will was starting to feel better.

"I just need to make a little cash. I'll do it if you really need me."

Will gave John a hug. "I appreciate it man."

Will walked back to the kitchen and helped with the closing chores.

John just sat there quietly. *What just happened? I think I was made a manager. That was so weird. I think he set me up. He must've seen the giant word on my forehead—SUCKER.*

It was so deliberate, the whole "Woe is me" bit. Regardless of what John thought he was the new manager of the Buona Vita.

He looked around the restaurant.

"I just need to keep my mouth shut." He didn't care if all of Provo heard him.

CHAPTER 18

The next forty-eight hours all ran together. Will was teaching John everything about the restaurant using the accelerated method.

"Dishwashers, Pedro, Juan, Jaime, Alejandro. This is John, the new manager. Mike is the Executive Chef, Debra does payroll." Will sounded like the guy who used to speak really fast and do commercials for the micro machines. John didn't have a second to himself.

At the end of the first day he stumbled home and collapsed on his bed. In the morning he woke up and realized he had slept on the floor. It was a blur.

John was a quick learner and he took everything in. He never thought managing a restaurant would be such a tedious and complex job. He had always thought managers delegated jobs to other people. *No. Wait a minute. That's what Will did to him.*

Most nights in the restaurant John was on the floor taking care of customers and keeping an eye on the servers. Now he knew why Will was always hovering. John found himself worrying about everything just like Will had. Once he realized what he was doing, he tried to back off. There was one problem. A majority of the servers needed someone to check up on them. It was that simple.

John did have a different method than Will. He would talk to the servers when they were having some down time.

He looked around. He was in charge, but all he wanted to do was serve tables, make a few bucks and that would be the end of it. He noticed Will wasn't around as much as he used to be. John thought maybe Will and his girlfriend could now spend some quality time together.

John was actually a very considerate guy. He was known to have loaned money to friends and never ask for it back. He was a simple guy with simple expectations.

It was a good night for the restaurant. It was one of the better nights since it opened. Will showed up at about nine o'clock to look at the sales.

"I'm impressed. You're a natural." Then came the pat on the back.

"Don't get any ideas. This is only temporary, very temporary until I can find something else." John was starting to get worried. What had he done?

As the restaurant closed for the night, two of the female servers were at each other's throats. John ran over to separate them.

"What's going on here?"

Silvia, the brunette server from Brazil was the first to talk. "Look. All I know is Rebecca has been talking about me."

Rebecca with her innocent face looked surprised to hear the accusation.

"Rebecca, did you say anything about Silvia?" John asked.

"No. I'm not like that." Rebecca was serious and still trying to catch her breath.

"You didn't? Then why did I hear you did?" Silvia said still seething.

"I don't know Silvia. You just attacked me for no reason."

John stepped in. "Look. Shake hands and go finish your duties." He wanted to go home and forget about the entire day. He wondered what Charlotte was doing right at that moment.

Silvia and Rebecca shook hands.

"I'm sorry for attacking you," Silvia said sincerely. She had that Latin temper. John didn't ever want to get on her bad side.

Rebecca and Silvia parted ways and went back to cleaning the restaurant.

John walked over to Rebecca. "How's everything?"

"Good."

"I heard you saying stuff to the bus boys about Silvia earlier. Let me give you a word of advice. I wouldn't say anything about her to anyone again." John smiled.

"I didn't mean . . ."

John cut her off. "Next time I won't stop her. Think about that." He smiled again and walked away.

He didn't sign up for this. He was breaking up cat fights, filling orders, working on payroll, and everything else Will handed down to him.

John actually got out of the restaurant before ten. It was almost unheard of. He walked up to his apartment and noticed the steam coming off the Jacuzzi in the distance. Maybe it was just what the doctor ordered.

He threw off his work clothes and traded them in for board shorts.

The Jacuzzi was empty. Good. Finally John could get some peace and quiet. Maybe Charlotte had the same idea and they could meet at the Jacuzzi by happenstance, an unexpected rendezvous. It would be nice to see Charlotte but John was happy to be alone, resting his tired body in the steamy water. It felt great. He could feel the tension leave his body. He closed his eyes and simply enjoyed the solitude.

"Do you mind if I join you?" A woman's voice came out of nowhere.

John heard the voice. It wasn't Charlotte.

"Go ahead." He didn't care who it was.

"It's really hot." The woman put her foot in.

John opened his eyes. "Do you want me to turn it down?" He looked again at the woman. She slid into the Jacuzzi wearing a black bikini.

"I'm Rachel." She put out her hand.

"John." He tried to look right at her. What a body!

He closed his eyes again and tried to relax.

"Which one is the best jet?"

"Huh." John was still in awe of her body. She had a pretty face too.

"You know the most powerful jet. Which one?" Rachel just wanted some conversation.

"I think this one over here. John pointed it out and Rachel moved over to it but she took her time. She was doing it all on purpose so John would have to watch her.

"You have really pretty eyes," Rachel said and smiled at him.

"Thank you. I like your smile." John had to give a compliment in return. What were the odds he'd go out to the Jacuzzi and would be joined by one of the hottest girls he'd ever seen?

"Have you ever had someone suck your toes while you're in the Jacuzzi?"

John almost choked. "No." He was trying to avoid eye contact with her. He thought about Charlotte and then Rachel moved over to another jet, closer to him.

"I think this is the most powerful jet. So, where are you from?"

"L.A." John was short with his response.

Now Rachel was right next to John. He could feel her breathe. "So, what are you doing here?"

"It's a long story." John was definitely not going to go into it with her.

"I have a long attention span," Rachel said with a laugh.

John just wanted her to go away. His heart was beating fast and his hands were shaking a little under the water.

"Are you okay?" Rachel noticed his hands. She picked one up. "You have soft hands."

"It's nothing. I've been in here for a long time. I don't want to become a prune." John laughed nervously.

"Where do you live?" Rachel asked knowing exactly where he lived.

"Right over there in 160." John got out of the water. He picked up his towel and put on his gold LAKERS starter sweats and a sweatshirt. "It was nice meeting you."

"Can you hand me my towel?" Rachel wanted John to help her.

John paused. Then he picked up the towel. Rachel stepped out of the water, her body glistening as the steam rose up into the air. He looked at her again. Her body was absolutely perfect.

He put on his flip-flops and started back to his apartment.

"Do you mind if I sit in your apartment for a little while? Just to get warm and then I'll go home." Rachel turned on the charm. No man could resist her and John was first and foremost a man.

"Let me help you." John handed Rachel her clothes and waited for her to dress.

John opened the door to his apartment. "This place is kind of a mess."

Rachel went straight back to the bedrooms. "Which one is yours?"

"The one on the left." He turned up the heater. What he needed to do was turn down the heat.

When John entered his room Rachel was sitting on his bed drying off her hair. He was trying so hard to not give in. John closed his eyes. Think about Charlotte. Think about you together with her, arm in arm.

"I'm over here. Are you playing the Three Blind Mice Game? Go straight ahead. Warmer. Now two steps." Rachel started to laugh.

John opened his eyes. It was no use. He was so attracted to Rachel and she was giving him the green light.

"You lose. You opened your eyes." Rachel laughed again. Her laugh was contagious.

"I don't want to play." All of a sudden John's tone changed.

"Really?" Rachel moved toward him.

John put his hands on her shoulders. She won. He then ran one of his hands through her hair and started to caress her neck. Rachel closed her eyes and enjoyed the massage.

"You have strong hands." Rachel opened her eyes and moved closer to him, he to her, their lips met and it began.

He knew exactly what to do. He'd had plenty of make-out sessions but it had been awhile. He moved down and kissed her chin, down to her neck and nape, and back up to her lips. Rachel wanted more. So, John turned her head and kissed the back of her neck.

"Do you like that?" John wanted to make sure she was cool with everything.

"She was right." Rachel kissed him on the mouth again.

"What?"

"You do have nice lips." Rachel laughed again and bit his lip.

"Okay." John had no idea what she was talking about.

"Come here." Rachel held his face in her hands.

"You have nice lips, too." John wanted to give her a compliment in return but it was true Rachel had great kissable lips.

Rachel started to kiss John's neck. He felt tingles all over.

"Maybe we shouldn't—"

"Shut up." Rachel put two fingers over his mouth and let out another laugh.

"Fine." John started to kiss her back and wrestle with her on his bed.

They continued the onslaught of kisses for about two hours. It was a Mormon make-out session. They never went past kissing each other on the mouth, neck, or ears.

It was 3 a.m. and John wasn't tired anymore. Rachel gave him one last final sweet kiss and walked out the door. He noticed her hair smelled like strawberries.

"I'll call you."

"You better." John could hear Rachel yell in the distance.

John smiled. He kind of needed that. He shut the door, locked it, turned off the lights, and went to bed.

He sat on his bed and then the guilt began to mount. He didn't do anything wrong with Rachel. It was that he kissed another girl at all. He wanted to be faithful to Charlotte. John knew that was ridiculous. Charlotte was engaged to someone else.

Rachel caught John at a weak moment. He was tired, over-worked, and simply vulnerable.

John stayed up for two hours trying to validate his decision to make-out with Rachel. *Charlotte's kissing Brian*, he thought. *Yeah, but it's her fiancé.* At about five o'clock John figured out why he had hooked up with Rachel. He was lonely. He thought it was a pathetic reason but at least he was being honest with himself. John hadn't kissed a girl for at least three months. That was a major drought for him. He was due. And Rachel satisfied that need. John knew it was shallow to think that way. There was nothing he could do. It was the way it worked.

Deep down John knew it was a mistake to hook up with Rachel. Maybe a mistake he would never live down. John finally tired and knew the next day would be another busy, unpredictable day.

CHAPTER 19

John woke up various times during the remaining hours of the night. He would sit up and debate in his head whether he should've done something different with Rachel. Maybe he could've driven her to her apartment. He knew he wasn't definitely thinking straight when he made the decision to let her inside his place.

He had to clear his head, do something. Back in L.A., John liked to run hills for exercise. So he put on some thermals, a beanie, a sweatshirt, gloves, and his gold Lakers starter sweats and headed out the door. There was light snow but John wasn't worried since he was all bundled up.

John decided to run right across the Seven Peaks Golf Course and then run straight up the mountain behind it. It sounded like a good plan.

He could feel the cold on his face. He wasn't sure how cold it was, just that it was cold. He was used to sunny skies and he was a wuss about the cold. The golf course was desolate and covered with snow. John continued over it and then followed a golf cart trail up toward the mountain.

John stopped to look up at his first hill. He could see the top. Back in California he liked to do high knees all the way to the top of the hills, but he'd never run in mountains there.

He dug in his feet, took a deep breath, pumped his arms and tried to lift his knees up. Maybe it was the wet ground but he wasn't having much luck. Finally he made it to the top.

"That was easy." John looked up at his next challenge, at least three times the size of the previous hill.

John thought he could see the top but wasn't sure. He took a couple of deep breaths and headed up the hill. John's face was now getting colder and his legs were starting to burn but he continued on.

He was not a quitter, never had been. John loved a challenge. Maybe that's why he was drawn to Charlotte. He wondered if he would be so "gung ho" to go after her if she wasn't engaged. He couldn't answer that question. John knew guys were weird like that. If something is too easy it isn't worth it.

John bent down to take in another deep breath. He was feeling winded. In his excitement to run hills he had forgotten about the altitude change. The air was thinner up here. He continued upward. Nothing was going to stop him from reaching the top. It seemed like the hill went on forever. John could feel his heart racing and his lungs burning.

He looked down at where he had come from. It was a long way down. John couldn't be deterred. He dug deeper and continued up the hill. At times he lost his footing but found a way to stay on his feet. Once again he glanced up to where he could make out the top. There was a big rock marking the spot. John could sit there and take a break before he went back down.

John wasn't sure if he would ever run hills during winter in Provo again. That didn't matter. He couldn't turn around. Well, he could but he didn't want to. He looked up and gathered strength. *Come on John, dig deeper. Don't give up. It will be worth it. Pump your legs. There's no pain. You feel warm. You feel good. You're the man.*

His legs were moving even slower now but at least they were moving. He looked down at his feet, begging them to keep going. The higher he went, the harder it was to get a deep, full breath.

Finally he reached the rock and sat down. He pumped his fist. He was happy. He had made it. He looked around and then came a smile. He couldn't believe he had done it. He felt great. He was on top of the world.

Then, he turned to look up and realized he was only at the middle of the last hill. The top was still about fifty feet or so away.

He started to laugh. John was alone on top of a hill in the cold, actually on the middle of a hill, thinking about the irony of the situation. *The story of my life. I'm always stuck in the middle. I'm never at the bottom. No, not me. I'm able to progress higher than that. Why couldn't this have been the top? Is this some kind of a joke? And what good would it do to make it to the top? Would I even make it? What would it prove? I don't think my body can make it another step.*

John stood up and looked down. His stomach was growling and his face was almost frozen. He turned around to face the nemesis.

"I was going to run to the top of this hill. Why not," he said aloud.

He rolled his neck, shook out his legs and dug deeper than possibly he had ever dug before in his life.

It was a sight to see John's ascension. At times he scratched, pulled, and even crawled on all fours on his way up. He fell a couple of times but picked himself back up.

The whole time John looked straight ahead and never back down. He wasn't going to stop until he reached the top. John's entire body was aching and the cold didn't help. He felt a little cramp in his left leg but shook it off.

He kept moving, digging deep as the top came closer. Finally, he was close enough to know he would make it and his face lit up sensing the victory.

John ran the last ten feet to the top like Sylvester Stallone running the steps in *Rocky*. He made it and this time it was the top.

"I own you!" John screamed and threw his arms into the air. He conquered it. He did a little dance.

The fatigue caught up with him quickly. He was spent. He tried to suck in air but instead just sat there.

And then he turned around to make sure he was on top of the hill. He was but another hill stared down at him.

"I'll get you next time." John said as he smiled and looked out at the prize. He could see all of Provo, most of Orem, Payson, and the surrounding cities. He could also see Utah Lake. What a vision. It was worth it.

John knew nothing came easy in life. No free lunches. Maybe that was the problem with "The Plan." He thought it would all happen like clockwork. Well, he was wrong.

He sat there for a spell re-charging his battery and thinking about what he had learned. You can never get anything unless you sacrifice and work for it. If you work for it you value it that much more. It's the struggles that build character and resolve. Even if you hit the wall. The wall is just there to remind you to keep going. And look at this view. *I earned this view. I would have never seen it if I had stopped mid-way.*

John took one last look at the panoramic view. He was pleased with himself. Charlotte had awakened him from his slumber of disenchantment. Regardless of what happened with him and Charlotte he was a changed man forever. He liked the transformation that was taking place.

He still felt guilty about Rachel but he knew he'd be stronger next time and wouldn't let it happen again. At least not until he knew Charlotte had chosen Brian over him.

Before John turned to go down he took a good look at the

hills he had climbed. It was more like a mountain. John knew he had conquered the mountain. He knew he could do anything. And he knew he wanted to be with Charlotte more than ever. He'd go all the way, and then some, to have her.

CHAPTER 20

Wake up early, go to the restaurant and get everything ready for another business day. That was John's routine, and he dreaded it.

He decided he didn't like working at all. He had always hoped one day a rich relative would appear and give him some valuable land or just a million dollars in cold, hard cash. The reality was John didn't have any extremely rich relatives so he had to work.

Getting a restaurant ready was a time consuming and painful process. Sometimes servers didn't show, so he'd have to call others at a moment's notice and Will was nowhere in sight. He'd left the restaurant in the capable hands of John. On top of it all, people were calling for John about the restaurant. John felt like he was in a box and all the sides were closing in around him.

John felt like putting an ad in the paper. It would read: "Indentured servant for sale or rent; you chose. Caucasian, 27, 6'2", brown hair, blue eyes, and a hard worker. He likes to work a lot for nothing and will do anything you want with a smile. He goes by John but you can re-name him."

He knew he'd become a bit of a pushover. When he was younger he was doing the pushing; now the tables were turned and he was being pushed.

John noticed that Silvia, the Brazilian had a thing for him. She'd always wink at him when she passed by. It was the last thing he needed in his life. It was a weird situation; however, because John had served his mission in Brazil. He'd always found the Brazilian women to be quite attractive and sexy.

Silvia was no exception. She had olive skin, strong features, long legs, and a flat stomach.

He stopped himself right there. *Don't even think about it?* Nothing was going to happen between him and Silvia, unless she put him in a headlock and forced him to kiss her. The funny thing is he could see her doing it. She was beautiful and yet very tough. John couldn't even consider it an option. No rationalization, absolutely none.

Lunch was always busy at Buona Vita. The masses loved the lunch specials and there was a thirty-minute wait.

John was walking around the restaurant keeping his eye on everything when Hope and Nate sat down.

Nate took the day off school and they left Luke with a friend. It was the first time in over three months they'd been out together. They held hands over the table. Hope and Nate were very much in love. Nate kissed the tops of each of Hope's hands and she blushed. They were representative of a third of the BYU student body.

At BYU, one third were married, one third were single women, and one third were single men. So, about ten thousand people were married at BYU.

Kurt was their server. He brought them water and bread to start off. Hope and Nate were still looking at the menu. Kurt told them he'd be right back.

John met Kurt on his way to the kitchen. "How are the guests?"

"Good."

"Do you need anything?"

"Did I ever tell you how weird it is that now you're my boss?" Kurt was being honest. When Kurt served John a couple of weeks earlier he wasn't sure if he liked him at all. And now he was his boss.

"Now you've told me. If you're cool with it then so am I."

"I'm cool."

"Then we're cool." John smiled. He was getting good at being the manager.

Will walked in wearing a beanie and talking on his cell. "Look. I'm happy with who I have. Thank you."

"Hey Will. Where have you been?"

"Man. Does it ever stop?"

"Do you have a second. I need to talk to you about some stuff."

"Can it wait?"

"No Will. It can't."

Will looked down at his watch. "All right. Shoot."

"Our bread supplier can't get the bread here by next week. We're almost out."

"Call Phil Johnson. He'll give you alternate suppliers. What else?"

"Some of the servers aren't showing up for shifts. And Silvia and Rebecca almost got in a fight the other day."

"If people don't show up, fire 'em. Who won the fight?" Will was so nonchalant. It almost made John ill.

"I stopped it." John was completely overwhelmed.

Will patted John on the back. "You're doing fine. I've got to go."

"Where are you going?"

"Snowboarding."

"With your girlfriend? How are things?"

"No. We broke up. She said I never listened to her. I'm going with this hot blonde chick I met at Harrio's last Saturday."

"Will, was that the Saturday you said you were sick?" John thought he had him.

"I'll see you tomorrow." Will headed out the door.

"Great. That's just great." John knew it was one thing to be played, but it was another thing entirely to have the person tell you point blank you've been played.

Silvia rushed over to him. "Are you okay?" She put her right hand on his shoulder.

"I'm fine. Just get away." John wanted to quit. He wanted to abandon the restaurant, but he knew he couldn't do that.

John looked at the tables. Everybody appeared to be happy. He walked around to get a better look.

"How are we doing today folks?"

Nate was the first one to turn his head. "John? Look Hope it's John."

"Hi." John was caught like a deer in headlights.

"What are you doing here?" Nate had no idea.

"Hope, how are you doing?" Hope didn't even budge. John tried again. "Hope, why won't you talk to me? She turned her face from him.

"She doesn't want to talk to you." Nate was the master of the obvious.

"What did I do?"

"Tell him there's nothing to talk about." Hope passed the message to Nate.

"She said . . ."

"I know what she said. I'm right here. I must've done something." John was already tired of the game.

"Tell him I'm upset at him." Hope wasn't going to quit the game just yet.

Before Nate could relay the message John jumped in. "I know." He smiled at Nate.

"Ask him what he's doing at this restaurant." Sometimes Hope was childish when she was upset.

"I'm the manager here."

"Tell him I heard he was working for a computer company in Salt Lake."

Nate folded his arms.

"Who told you that?" John asked.

Then Hope turned to look at John. "Charlotte."

"Charlotte?"

"Isn't that what you told her when you ran into her last week jogging?"

"How do you know that?" He was dumbfounded. Was she following him?

"First, why am I upset? Well, let me think. My brother moves to Provo, doesn't call, doesn't even tell me. Then I have to hear it from my engaged friend that he's stalking."

"Oh no. Please tell me you didn't tell her I knew she was engaged before our first meeting." John was starting to feel the heat.

Nate started to laugh. Hope gave him a dirty look and he dipped his head and began working on his pasta.

"No. I didn't tell her. And obviously you lied to her. She thinks it's all a coincidence."

"Thank you," John said, grabbing Hope's hand.

"John, I just want to know one thing. What are you doing?" Hope was determined to know.

John looked at her and smiled. "Have you ever made a mistake in your life, something you wish you would've done differently?"

"We all have."

"Well, I made a mistake a long time ago with Charlotte. I ignored her and her feelings for me." He thought it made perfect sense.

"I told you she had a crush on you a long time ago."

"Did you know I kissed her once after my mission?"

"Of course." Hope thought John was so clueless.

"How?" John managed to ask.

"Charlotte told me. And then she said you didn't want to be with her."

"It wasn't like that. Forget it. It was so long ago." John was becoming flustered. It bothered him that his little sister was in his business. His entire life she'd known everything going on with him. It bugged him. She was like a master of espionage.

"So, answer my question. What are you doing?" Nate was smiling again.

"I don't know. I don't know."

Hope looked him straight in the eye. "You'd better find out." Then she started to eat her pasta. "This is really good."

And the conversation was over. That's how it always was with Hope. She'd trap you in intense dialogue and then let it go when she was done with you.

"Thanks. Do you want any dessert? It's on me." John offered. He loved Hope. She understood him.

"Sure. Have any cheesecake?" Hope asked, done with the interrogation.

"Raspberry swirl or plain?"

"Raspberry swirl."

John started to walk away.

"I love you, John," Hope said. She just wanted the best for him.

Nate grabbed Hope's hand. "I love it when you're tough."

Hope grabbed him right back. "I know honey. I know."

"I mean, just the way you talked to him. It was amazing,"

"Are you going to eat anymore?" Hope asked. She liked Nate's pasta better. She took a big bite.

John sat in the office. He knew what he was doing. And he knew what he wanted. He couldn't tell Hope. He couldn't tell anyone.

He was afraid to wear his heart on his sleeve. He'd been burned before. Heidi Robinson broke his heart. She was a beautiful, stylish blonde girl he knew from Huntington Beach. They met at FHE (Family Home Evening) for the Huntington

Beach VIII Ward.

John had picked her out of the crowd because of her style and winning smile. Heidi was sitting by herself on a table. John had never seen her before but he'd watched her all night.

The door was open, so he took it and stepped up to the plate. He sat down next to her. At first there was an awkward silence. John looked over at her. She noticed and smiled back at him. He could feel the mutual attraction. He slowly moved closer to her.

"Hi. I don't know you," John said.

"No, you don't." Heidi smiled again.

"I'm John Edwards. Are you new?" He put his hand out. They shook hands. John noticed how soft and delicate her hands were.

"Heidi Robinson. I'm kind of new. Well, not really."

"So, which one is it?" John tried to be witty.

"Whichever one you want." Touché. John liked the girl already. She had an intangible quality called sass. And he liked girls with sass.

John and Heidi saw each other every single day for almost a month. And every time she was with him she'd say how happy she was and how wonderful she felt. He was on cloud nine. Every moment of his day had Heidi in it.

They even went to church and sat together, holding hands. They talked about having kids, raising a family, and what their lives would be like down the road.

John even did the cardinal sin of dating. He told friends he was going to marry Heidi. He knew it could jinx everything but he didn't care. He loved Heidi, or at least he thought he was in love.

One day it all turned. John went over to her house to celebrate the anniversary of the first time they met. The night before Heidi had kept trying to get John to tell her where they were going to celebrate their first month anniversary. He had refused to tell her. He knocked on her door and her brother answered and said she wasn't there. He called her later that night and the next day. She wouldn't return his phone calls. He thought something must've happened to her. John talked to Heidi's mother who assured him that she was okay. He had no idea what happened or what was going on and pathetically left a dozen messages on her phone, notes on her car, and at her work. What had happened?

John went to church on Sunday hoping to see her so they could talk. She wasn't there. She wasn't anywhere. It was driving him crazy. He looked at the poetry he'd written her and simply shook his head. He couldn't do anymore. John became depressed. He didn't want to eat. He called in sick at work and slept whole days.

He began to realize his pattern of depression and finally decided to move on. Something had to change. That experience taught John that he was a hopeless romantic, a lovesick fool. It was his disease, his curse. He had to forget Heidi and there was only one way. He kept himself totally busy everyday working out, swimming, surfing, anything to fill his day. And it was working.

Then one full moon Heidi knocked on his door. He opened the door and there she was smiling at him. The visit was quick. She apologized for how she had acted. John didn't care he just wanted to be with her. Heidi told him they needed to be friends. That statement pierced John's heart. He was crushed. She told him why she hadn't been at church. Heidi told him she'd been inactive for the last four years and the first time she'd done anything with Mormons was the FHE where she met him.

John held her in his arms. "I don't care. It's in the past."

"I need time, John," Heidi said. She was about to cry.

"Do you believe in the gospel?" John had to know.

"I've had this boyfriend off and on for like six years. Well, he showed up again two weeks ago."

"That was when you wouldn't see me?" He knew where the conversation was going.

"He's not Mormon. And we've been very intimate. It was pretty much a physical relationship. I didn't know how to tell you this."

"Now he's back in the picture." John was losing it.

"I know it will never work out but we have this history. John, are you okay?"

John wasn't okay. One single tear fell down his cheek. He wiped it away before Heidi could see it.

"I'm fine. I just thought . . ."

"I know what you thought." Heidi held his hand. "I love being with you. I'm just confused."

"What do you want?" John tried a different tactic.

"I don't know." The words fell softly off Heidi's lips.

John knew people said "I don't know" because they were afraid of the real outcome.

Now he was afraid. He was definitely afraid Charlotte would choose Brian over him. It was that fear that kept him from spilling his guts to Hope. He wanted to tell her everything, how he felt about Charlotte, and how he'd always felt about her. He knew she wouldn't completely understand. He didn't think anyone would understand. Some days he didn't know if he understood himself.

Once again he thought about Charlotte reaching out to him and pulling him to her. She could make him whole. Charlotte could make him happy forever.

CHAPTER 21

It was one of the hardest decision John had ever made. He decided he had to call on Charlotte. He knew where she lived. In fact, he'd passed by her apartment everyday in his car. And every single time he wanted to walk up and knock on her door. He waited. He was patient. Now the time had come.

John stood outside looking up at the number on her door, 142. He rang the doorbell. He rang it again. He could see the peephole and didn't want her to see him and not open the door, so he turned his back to the door.

He heard the locks open and turned around to face the door. It was Charlotte. They looked at each other. Both were quiet, but they looked at each other like they wanted to say everything going through their heads.

"Hi." Charlotte was the first to break the silence.

"I don't really know anyone else in Provo." John smiled.

"Do you want to come in?"

"Sure." John walked in. He looked around at everything. Finally he was inside her apartment, just him and Charlotte.

"Want anything to drink?" Charlotte was looking in the kitchen for a glass already.

"I don't want to be any trouble."

"You're no trouble John."

"I'll have some water," John decided and cleared his throat.

Charlotte came back with the water, handed it to him, and sat down on the couch across from him.

"How are you doing?" John wanted to spend as much time as possible with her. So, he proceeded with the small talk.

"I'm good. You?"

"I'm good too." John took another sip from the water. He was nervous.

"Good." Charlotte knew they were both uncomfortable.

"Charlotte, have you ever thought about the night on the beach?" John went for it.

"What night?"

"I'd just returned from my mission. We went to a dance with Hope and then we drove down to the cove. And we kissed." John's palms were sweating. He wiped them on his jeans.

"We kissed?" Charlotte said, trying to dodge the question.

"We kissed." John stood up. He was animated. "Yes. We kissed. And there was something there. Something I'd never felt before." He walked over to her and sat down on the couch beside her. He picked up her hand. "What I need to know is if you felt it too."

Charlotte looked in his eyes. She squeezed his hand. Their faces moved toward each other and their lips were inches apart. Their lips moved even closer, feeling each other breathe.

The doorbell rang. Charlotte moved away, looked at John and then at the door. "I'd better get that." Charlotte was a little worked up. She stood up, shook it off, and opened the door.

Brian came in and gave her a kiss on the cheek. "How are you, sweetie? I'm starving. Do you want to order take-out?"

Charlotte smiled. Then Brian noticed John sitting on the couch.

"Brian, this is John. He's an old friend. John, this is Brian my fiancé."

John stood up. Brian walked over to him. "How you doing?" They shook hands.

Brian sensed something was wrong, but he trusted Charlotte.

"I'd better be going." John stood up to leave.

"Did I interrupt something?" Brian addressed Charlotte.

"No. Nothing really. Just catching up. John is Hope's brother."

"Hope? Right. Hope's brother." Now it was registering in Brian's brain. He'd heard about John.

"We'll just catch up later. Think about what I asked you." John shook Charlotte's hand. He wanted to kiss her so bad. "Nice meeting you Brian."

John reached for the door but it was being opened from the other side. Rachel walked past John. He stopped cold in his tracks. He hoped Rachel was a figment of his imagination.

"Hey Charlotte, honey. I found the greatest tan jacket at Dillard's, on sale."

John wanted to leave but it was too late. Rachel saw him at the door.

"John, what are you doing here?"

He turned around and acted surprised. "Rachel. Hey."

"You guys know each other?" Charlotte was starting to suspect something.

"How long have we known each other, John? A little while, right?" Rachel was laughing inside; on the outside was a big cheesy grin.

"Yeah. We go back a little while." John was dying inside. He knew the Rachel make-out would come back to haunt him but never in his wildest dreams like this.

"You didn't know we were roommates?" Charlotte asked. She wanted answers.

"No. Rachel never told me you two lived together." John wanted to crawl into a hole but he had hope that Rachel would smooth things over.

"I don't know. I thought I did," Rachel said. She simply wanted to see John squirm.

Brian sat back and watched the drama unfold.

"No. I definitely didn't know. What a small world. Uh, that's kind of funny." John smiled awkwardly.

"Why is that funny?" Charlotte wasn't laughing. John didn't want to say anything else. "I guess I never realized how small the world really is," Charlotte said.

"I'll see you guys later. I've got to study. Good seeing you again, Johnny." Rachel walked over to John and gave him a hug and then disappeared into her room.

"Well, I'll be going now," John said and left.

Brian looked over at Charlotte. "Rachel studies?"

"Huh?" Charlotte's mind was somewhere else. She closed the door and sat down next to Brian on the couch.

It was a long walk back to John's apartment. He knew he had blown it. He could feel the door of opportunity slamming behind him. What were the odds? John could picture Charlotte's face when she heard Rachel and John were friends.

John pulled out his cell. He needed do something quick. He had started a fire and it was already out of control.

"Will. Hey, it's John. Look. I won't be able to work at the restaurant the next couple of days. I understand, but I have a bad situation here and it requires damage control quick."

John listened for a moment.

"Listen to me Will. I've got a lot going on in my life right now, too. What do you mean you can't believe I'm doing this to you? I can't do this right now? Goodbye Will." And John hung up. He wanted to chuck the phone on the ground and jump on it over and over again. John wished that he could find an old abandoned house that was scheduled to be demolished, then he could tear it down by himself one brick at a time.

His cell phone rang. It was Will.

"Yeah." John put the phone to his ear.

"I'm going to have to let you go." Will was totally serious.

"What? Are you kidding me? Fine. I don't care," John replied. He was beside himself.

He hung up the phone. He wanted to cancel his life. Then he remembered he'd done that already by moving to Provo and trying to win Charlotte's affection. His life was a mess. He had tried but at every turn his plans had turned into a complete and unexpected disaster.

A few minutes earlier John and Charlotte had their eyes locked and their lips had been moving toward each other. Then Brian, the antithesis of John, had come waltzing in, followed by the stand-up comedy act of Rachel. What a day! John laughed sarcastically. It's all about timing. And he knew his timing was always bad.

John wanted to scream so all of Provo could hear him say how much of an idiot he was. It didn't matter.

He'd probably be ignored. And he didn't want sympathy. He only wanted that moment back when Charlotte's soft, waiting lips breathed on his.

He thought about packing up his car and going back to California, never to be seen in Provo again. He'd been walking a long time. He suddenly noticed that he'd passed his apartment. He turned around and headed back to his place.

John wanted to throw in the towel but he knew he would never get over it if he did. There was something inside John that wouldn't let him quit. He was in LOVE with Charlotte and he probably always had been. And he knew if he stopped trying to win Charlotte he'd regret it for the rest of his life.

The cell phone rang. Once again, it was Will.

"John. I've been thinking. How many days do you need?"

"You fired me." John couldn't care less.

"I know I was a little rash."

"Rash? Rash? I've been running your restaurant. And then you fired me like a minute ago and now you call back to say you're rash. Are you nuts?" John was now angry, not completely angry at Will, but at the entire situation he found himself in.

"Hey. You have every right to be angry. How many days? Come on buddy."

"Three days."

"Three days. I don't know if we can manage that." Will had hoped for less.

"Three days. I'm not going to compromise." John was starting to pace. He didn't really want to go back, ever. It was the principle of the thing. Will had fired him for no reason.

"You drive a hard bargain. Three days."

"See you later, Will."

"Enjoy yourself, man."

He wanted to cuss out Will but instead refrained and hung up the phone.

John had handpicked the best bed, tested it out, made it, and now had to sleep in it.

Three days. John knew he had three days to prove his love to Charlotte. And three days to clean up the mess he'd made. Not a lot of time but at least that was one thing he did have, time.

CHAPTER 22

It was between Charlotte and Rachel. Who should he call first? He decided to call Rachel first. John had to know the reason behind the sabotage.

He told her to meet him at Denny's. Denny's was the perfect place. John and Rachel would be inconspicuous among Goth chicks, white trash, and other creatures of the night. John knew he'd have to wait for Rachel and looked around Denny's, reminiscing.

At one time Denny's was the place to go after youth dances in Southern Cal. All of John's sweaty friends would look at each other and echo the same refrain, "Denny's!"

John always ordered the French Slam with extra bacon and eggs sunny side-up and wheat toast. It was John's senior year at high school and he was kind of the leader of the crowd. Most of his buddies ordered water and a gang of lemons and made their own lemonade. His sister Hope always got a large serving of something and never finished it. John would tell her not to order anything because she never finished it. Every time Hope would say, "I will this time." John calculated that they'd eaten at Denny's approximately 250 times after church dances or other occasions and the number of times Hope had eaten the entire meal was a big FAT zero.

He couldn't argue with her because sometimes she paid for him too.

That particular night Hope ordered the "Moons Over My Hammy" (John always thought that was a great name). Charlotte ordered some French fries and a strawberry shake.

She was always there looking at him. Why was he so blind?

John was busy finishing off his French Slam and helped Hope with her "Moons." Everybody was having a good time. There were no worries. No bills to pay. High school was low stress. There were absolutely no expectations. Just young teenagers having fun being teenagers.

Amanda was the girl John had met that night at the dance. She lived in Anaheim Hills next to a house Arnold Swartzenegger was looking at (that's what she had said). They danced the whole night together and then went outside.

In those days John liked to use one particular line. "It's kind of hot in here. Do you want to go outside to cool off?"

He used it that night on Amanda. They went outside and John began to massage her neck and tell her how beautiful she was and how great she smelled. Then he'd massage her shoulders and move one of his hands onto her face. He had a simple test that he used to see if the girl was interested. He'd touch the girl's lips with his finger. If she reacted to the touch by kissing his finger then he knew he was good to go.

Amanda had kissed his finger and John had turned her around and kissed her on the mouth.

John was looking at her and he felt like the man. Amanda was pretty hot. The exchange was sudden and then it was over. He got her digits and they went their separate ways.

"How are you doing?" Charlotte asked. She had smiled at him, looking over her menu. Her crush had been building.

"Good. Did you have fun tonight?" John asked.

"Yeah. Did you?" Charlotte wanted more time to spend with him.

"It was good. You meet anybody?" he required.

And she said, "Sort of. You?"

"Kind of." John smiled and put the number away.

He had looked around and could see that everybody was

done eating and that they had paid. Then he went over to his friend Pete. "Who's going to do 'The Rooster' tonight?" John asked, wanting to recruit someone.

"I don't know if we should do it at this Denny's," Pete said, always trying to be John's conscience.

John insisted. "We have to. I'll do it. Just get everybody out to the cars and give me a head start."

"All right."

"The Rooster" was a silly thing that John and his buddies did for fun at every Denny's restaurant they'd been to. All you needed for "The Rooster" was a coffee bar and thankfully every Denny's had one right near the door.

John had actually invented "The Rooster" one day when he was listening to *Alice in Chains* (one of the great Seattle bands before they all became trendy). The song went something like, "Yeah, here come the Rooster. Yeah, here come the Rooster." Later on he'd learned that the song was about Vietnam. Well, "The Rooster" was an impersonation of sorts. Timing was the most important thing about "The Rooster." Some of his friends would already be in their cars, and others would be on their way out the door. John would look for the "go sign." That night he could hardly wait for the fine people of Hacienda Heights to meet "The Rooster." John jumped up on the coffee bar. He looked around and then got down in Rooster pose and let out the loudest "rooster" noise you've ever heard. It was different at every Denny's. Sometimes people laughed, sometimes they got angry and started yelling. At that particular Denny's in Hacienda Heights it was a smorgasbord of emotions. Most of the people stopped eating and looked dumbfounded. What had just happened? Was that a Rooster? I think I heard a Rooster!

John jumped down and headed out the door with a big grin on his face. He couldn't wait up there much longer.

The manager came running outside. "I'm going to call the

police!" he shouted. John hopped into the waiting car and they were off. They all drove away dying of laughter. Throughout the drive home everyone had given his or her own take on what it was like inside Denny's. Someone even said they could hear "The Rooster" all the way out in the car.

"How many is that now, John?" Pete asked as he drove the getaway car.

"That makes twenty," John said and couldn't help but laugh some more.

"Twenty. You're the man." Pete had started busting up.

"You should have seen the manager's face. He looked like the old guy who owned the amusement park from Scooby Do. I'll get you kids," John was in rare form. John, Pete, Charlotte, and Hope continued in their hilarious fit of laughter.

"You're crazy, John," Charlotte said. She had looked at him with a special gaze.

He smiled back with that cool grin. "I know."

John didn't know why he did "The Rooster" at all. Maybe because he didn't drink, smoke, do drugs, or have sex, so he had to be creative in other ways. Or it could've been because of the rush he felt whenever he was on top of the coffee bar. It made him feel invincible. It was when he jumped down that it was all about survival. John had never got caught once. He really didn't know what they could do to him. He made a rooster noise on a coffee bar. Maybe disturbing the peace, but they couldn't throw the book at him.

John had done "The Rooster" at the Provo Denny's ten years earlier when he was there on a ski trip with his buddies— he actually did it twice, two nights back to back. All in all John had done "The Rooster" in five states including New Jersey and at over thirty different Denny's locations. He laughed just thinking about it. Those were the days.

John looked around at the Denny's in Provo. Yes, Denny's had memories and Charlotte was always in them. He knew

Rachel would be late—she just seemed the type. His French Slam was already in front of him and half gone. He wasn't going to do "The Rooster" that night. John stopped doing "The Rooster" right before he left on his mission. Never again would Denny's see "The Rooster." Of course there were copycats but John knew he created the winged, screaming creature of havoc. "The Rooster" was his baby forever.

Finally Rachel showed up and sat down. She had on tight faded blue jeans and a black shirt with sparkles.

"Hi. Am I late?" Rachel winked at him. "What's the matter?"

"I like the French Slam. What do you want?"

"Can I look at the menu?"

"Nope." John took the menu from Rachel. "Debra." John liked to call the servers by the name on their nametags—it always surprised them that he paid attention.

"She wants the French Slam." He turned to Rachel. "With bacon, right?" Rachel nodded her head sheepishly. "With bacon and eggs sunny side-up."

"I don't like eggs sunny side-up."

"Yes, you do." John handed the menu to Debra. "I think that's it. Thanks." Debra walked away.

He took a sip of his water. "I almost ate one French Slam waiting for you and that's what I like. So, if you don't finish it I will." John was in charge.

Rachel was put in her place. She wanted to pout but it'd do no good. She could feel the momentum switch. There were no more flirtatious winks or smiles. She was stoic.

"So, why did I ask you to come here?" John tested her.

Rachel was slow to respond. "I wondered."

"Did I do something to you?" John asked.

"What do you mean?" Rachel mused.

"The other night. You totally planned that, right?"

"Kind of."

John laughed. "There's no kind of. It was deliberate, premeditated. And that must mean you know about Charlotte and me?"

"Charlotte told me a little about your history." Rachel was feeling comfortable again.

"What did she tell you?" John questioned.

"Everything." Rachel smiled at him. She couldn't help it.

John stopped the questioning for a second. "I wasn't waiting for that. So, why did you do it?"

"Do what?"

"Come on. Don't play Miss innocent. You seduced me into making out with you." John was in her face.

Rachel's face changed, like flipping a switch. "Excuse me. It takes two to tango."

John could feel the tables turning.

Debra put the French Slam in front of Rachel. "Thank you." She picked up the syrup and poured it on the French toast.

"I understand. What I'm saying is you didn't tell me you were Charlotte's roommate," John said.

"You didn't ask." Rachel took a big bite.

"That's not fair."

"When did you want me to tell you, before or after you were biting my neck?" Rachel took another bite of the French toast. "This is really good."

"I'm not a bad guy," John said, trying to plead his case.

"Were you attracted to me?"

"Yes. You're beautiful." John put Rachel in the top ten of the hottest girls he'd kissed. He bumped Lori Simon out (John believed every guy had a top ten list of the hottest girls they'd been with. It worked like the high score on a video game. And Rachel was in the top ten, maybe fifth.)

"And I thought you were attractive. That's it. It was just a make-out. It didn't mean anything," Rachel countered.

"Right," John replied. He had been wrong about Rachel.

Rachel dipped her toast in the golden center of the sunny side-up eggs and took a bite. "This is really good. Look. Charlotte told me you were a good-looking guy, you were new in town and had great lips."

John smiled. That comment padded his already inflated ego. "Great lips."

"Wait. No. She said nice lips."

"Nice lips. That's good too, right?" John was totally seeking confirmation.

John was feeling like the man. He wanted to stand up on the coffee bar and blast off the best "Rooster" ever, but that would be stupid.

"Can you do something for me?" John asked politely.

"What, honey?"

"I really care about Charlotte and I think she likes me too. When you talk to her about this . . ." He took another gulp of the water. "Will you tell her what you told me, that I had no idea who you were? Would you do that, please?"

Rachel laughed. "You kill me, John. I really like your style. You're such a freak." She kissed him on the cheek. "I'll do it."

John smiled, knowing he had detoured a potential disaster. He kind of dug Rachel and he didn't tell her then but she had nice lips too. "It was only a make-out." John only wished it was that simple.

Chapter 23

Brian picked up Charlotte and they drove through Provo Canyon toward Sundance. They didn't say a word to each other.

Then she smiled at him. "How was your day, honey?"

He smiled back. "Good." Charlotte had no idea where they were going.

Brian's Tahoe climbed up the mountain and then stopped at a clearing. The view was gorgeous. Trees went on for miles and snow-covered mountains were all around.

"I've been thinking a lot lately, Charlotte."

Charlotte understood. "So have I."

"Well, the last couple of days have been weird and . . ."

"Brian, you know you can say anything to me." Charlotte said, holding his hand.

Brian had difficulty expressing his feelings. His family was also not very affectionate and it had taken awhile for him to become adjusted to how touchy-feely and affectionate Charlotte was. Brian's father, Walter, was a very busy man. He was the CEO of a Fortune 500 company back east. His job was his life; however he always made some time for the family. He was a good man and a Stake President. "I love you" was used sparingly in Brian's house growing up. He knew his family loved him but they just never said it often enough.

He had become more affectionate since dating Charlotte. In fact, the last time he talked to his dad he told him that he "loved him." His dad said, "What?" Brian just smiled and said it again, "I love you, Dad" and then hung up the phone.

Charlotte had changed Brian's life. He'd heard how people

say you should marry someone who will make you a better person. Well, she did just that for him. And he didn't want to lose her.

"I know about John."

"You do?" Charlotte was surprised to hear Brian be so blunt.

"Yes. I do. Hope told me all about him. And I think it's best . . ." Brian paused. He wanted to say everything just right.

"Yes?" Charlotte asked, waiting.

"I think it's best if you don't talk to him again. At one time you had feelings for him and if you were in my shoes you'd be asking me to do the same thing."

"You're right." Charlotte couldn't argue. It was a sound request. Maybe it was for the best. John was just a distraction.

"Good." Brian smiled. He felt like he was in control. (Women have a special gift to make a man feel like he runs the show. But the women are always pulling the strings behind the scenes. Brian was oblivious. Women are always in control. It wasn't Brian's fault. He only had a ten-year old sister. He didn't know any better.)

"Is that the reason why we're here?"

"No." Brian moved in on Charlotte.

He grabbed her passionately and they kissed. The kisses increased with impact and pleasure. Finally Brian pulled away.

Charlotte sat back and took a deep breath. *Where did that come from?* She looked over at him. Brian had made a transition, a big transition. It was Charlotte who had to always initiate the make-out sessions. Maybe it was because of John or because finally Brian had let go. She didn't care to ask Brian. He probably wouldn't know the difference. Brian took her hand and started to dig his thumb deep into her palm, massaging it. Charlotte was definitely not going to say anything. The whole surreal experience was making her hypothesize. *Has he been taking classes behind my back?*

Maybe it was much simpler than that. She remembered watching *The Saint* with Val Kilmer and Elisabeth Shue a couple of days earlier. Rachel always told her to have Brian watch that movie over and over again. Val Kilmer did something to women and in *The Saint* he was at his best. That had to be it. Brian must've watched *The Saint* at least a half dozen times and now he was imitating Val.

Brian started to kiss the back of Charlotte's neck. It was driving her crazy. Charlotte quit thinking about how and why. Brian had suddenly become passionate and she decided to just enjoy herself. She thought it was about time, anyway.

CHAPTER 24

John was taking a power nap. He awoke and looked at his watch. He'd been sleeping for six hours. He thought maybe everything was catching up with him. The long hours at the restaurant, the nights and days following Charlotte, and the constant struggle within himself wondering whether he was doing the right thing.

He was still a little drowsy but he had the answer, four words: Rage Against the Machine. John slipped "The Battle For Los Angeles" into the CD Player. "Testify" came in hard with Morello's guitar screaming and Zach's philosophic vocals filling in the pieces. John put Rage under the "angry music" category. Sometimes he was just in the mood to rock out hard and let all of his anger and disappointment flow out of him like a stream. Rage provided a cleansing of sorts. It actually removed those feelings out of his system.

Every time John heard a Rage song he thought about the first time he saw them play live. It was at Irvine Meadows during a Lollapallooza Tour (the tour founded by Perry Farrell of Jane's Addiction). The Beastie Boys, 311, Primus, and the Red Hot Chili Peppers were also on the bill.

The first song from Rage's set was "People Of The Sun." John waited quietly in the pit with Pete. Everyone in the pit was getting ready. The excitement was gleaming in their eyes. You could cut the suspense with a knife.

Zach walked out on stage with his dreads and it all began. The pit came alive as everyone jumped together up and down doing "the pogo" (like a pogo stick) or cruising around in a circle (like a whirlpool—everyone going the same way). Slam dancing was an art form. John liked to stay low in case guys from the outside of the pit tried to take cheap shots and hit him in the back. Pete was always in front of John. They watched out for each other. As the music continued to build, guys started to get knocked down to the ground. There's a bizarre brotherhood in a slam pit. If someone gets knocked down to the ground then everybody stops and tries to help them back up. It's kind of like a family that way.

A guy with a black beanie got plowed right in front of John. He went down hard. John stopped. He got hit from behind, but reached down and helped the guy to his feet and back into the fray.

"Thanks bro," was all that was said when someone was helped back to their feet.

John bounced right back into the whirlpool and flowed around doing his own style of funky arm movements. There was always a lot of pushing and shoving throughout the pit. Sometimes guys would stand in the middle and hit people as they went by. John took exception to that—it was weak. Usually he'd lower his shoulder and put that type of guy on his backside. The next time he would come around to them they weren't in the middle anymore.

A crazy phenomenon happened at the end of every Rage song. The whirlpool would dissolve as it became a free-for-all, people taking shots, slamming each other to the ground, guys getting lifted into the air and finding a rude awakening on the ground. Morello was jamming, faster and faster on his six-string. John followed the massive mosh (A mosh is when it's a free-for-all, bodies bouncing off each other like bumper cars).

John needed the release the day of the concert. He'd had one of those days he wanted to forget forever. Rage was just the medicine the doctor ordered. John pushed his way into the nucleus of the pit, where all of the action was taking place. He kept his hands in front of him pushing people out of the way and dodging possible collisions.

In the corner of his eye he saw a big guy, maybe 6'4" drop a shoulder into the back of a girl. The girl went flying and fell on the ground (girls' bodies aren't as susceptible to the hits as guys). Something clicked inside John's head. He rushed over to find the guy. He probably wasn't thinking, but what had happened was against all of the guidelines of a slam pit. You never take out a chick. NEVER. You protect them.

John imagined if the girl had been Hope or one of his other sisters. He swam through the crowd on a collision course with the perpetrator. John weighed about one-ninety at the time, giving the 6'4" guy at least thirty pounds on him but he didn't care. He increased his speed and met the guy seconds later. John lowered his shoulder, bent his knees, and exploded right into the guy like a rocket. He hit him right in the chest catching the guy off guard and sending him flying into a crowd and then down to the ground. The guy was dazed a little. John looked around and then continued in the mosh pit. He had a code of ethics. It came from his belief in the church and from his parents. John simply acted on his code. Those were the days.

John turned down "Testify" as he thought about his code of ethics. He'd thrown it by the wayside dealing with Charlotte. He knew she'd have to know the truth. He'd have to tell her he knew she was engaged all along.

Now he was awake. He pulled Rage from the CD player and replaced it with Vivaldi's "Four Seasons." What a contrast. John liked the two extremes. Music had a deep effect on him— Rage to wake up and Vivaldi to ponder. He wasn't an angry person at all. John was very happy. He knew he was blessed but like everyone else he wouldn't complain if he had more.

It was the age-old question: Can man ever have enough?

John wasn't sure he had the answer. He only wanted one thing, Charlotte. Would he want more if Charlotte chose him? He couldn't answer that question either. It was another bridge he'd have to cross. John had learned to not jump to conclusions or to expect something that wasn't already a reality. He wanted to spend an entire day with Charlotte. Then he could tell her how amazing and great she was. Maybe she could turn to him and reveal her true feelings. It would be like a surreal dream for him. He sat there and thought what it would be like. Charlotte would make him whole and a better man.

CHAPTER 25

John was nearing the end of his first day off. He was at the Del Taco eating two chicken soft tacos. His cell phone rang.

"Hello?"

"John." He knew the voice before she even said the "h" or the "n" in John.

"Charlotte, where are you?"

"At home. I know it's not cool to do this over the phone but well, the circumstances are complicated."

"What do you want to tell me?" John thought Charlotte was going to provide him with good news. Maybe Brian crashed into a tree, died on impact. That wasn't cool. John couldn't even believe he'd think such a thing. Or maybe better yet, Brian gave Charlotte an ultimatum about him and she said, "We're through!"

Charlotte took her time. She'd thought about it a lot. "I can't see you or talk to you anymore."

John responded before he heard her declaration. "Cool. I'm coming over."

"Did you hear me, John? I can't ever see you again. It's for the best."

It's for the best. That statement crippled him. He dropped his chicken soft taco. The tortilla came apart, spilling its contents all over the table in front of him.

"Charlotte. I just have to say something."

"What John?"

"I just want you to know what I'm thinking before you do this." John could hardly express himself. He wanted to say everything, every emotion, every feeling, and every thought.

"Oh, I want to know something. Did you really make-out with Rachel?"

John couldn't escape that one. "Did she tell you I had no idea you were roommates?"

"So what?" Charlotte was hurt regardless.

"I didn't know."

"John, I like you. We go back a long time but you have to understand. I'm getting married in two months."

"I thought it was in four months." John hoped he'd heard her wrong.

"Things change, John. Brian thought it was best to move up the date."

"Okay." He couldn't say anything else.

"Bye John. Please don't try to come see me. Take care." And Charlotte hung up.

John sat there, frozen. He didn't understand. He knew she had feelings for him. Did she love Brian more? Could Brian sense her sentiment for him?

It was nine o'clock. The end of DAY ONE. John wanted to sit in his apartment and sleep. He had the desire to sleep for days, maybe weeks, months, and years. Luckily there was a small part of him that took consolation in the way Charlotte talked to him. He thought about what she said, "Please don't try to come see me." John tossed that sentence around in his head. What if she was really saying: "Please. Don't try. Just come and see me." Deep down he knew she never said that but he believed it was implied. It had to be implied. It couldn't end like that—a phone call while he was eating 69-cent chicken soft tacos at Del Taco. No way!

The night was reaching a cold low, twenty-five degrees. John bundled up in a black scarf, black beanie, black gloves, and a heavy coat and headed out the door. He braved the cold on the long solitary walk three buildings down to Charlotte's.

The Belmont parking lot was full. John noticed a slow moving, old Ford sedan looking at every car with flashlights. They were finks, rats. Their job was to find out who didn't have a parking sticker for The Belmont. Then they'd call a tow truck or better known as *The Tow Truck Nazis*. A couple of John's friends had been booted there before, costing them fifty bucks each in the end. The Tow Truck Nazis were ruthless and acted without remorse. As John neared Charlotte's apartment he got a glimpse of a Tow Truck Nazi pulling into the parking lot. The tow truck stopped in front a Jeep Cherokee. John couldn't do anything. This was their job. He watched for a moment as the *Tow Truck Nazi* quickly hoisted the Jeep Cherokee away. In a weird sense that was exactly what John wanted to do to Charlotte. He wanted to cruise in and take her away.

He could see the light was on in her room but the blinds were shut. He walked up to her front door. He would just ring the doorbell. *No, wait,* he thought, *maybe I should knock. No, The doorbell is more discrete. So what, knocking is different.* John knew one thing for sure. He'd cover the peephole with his finger. He put his finger over the peephole and with his other hand knocked on the door. Then he pressed the doorbell. He could hear no movement inside. John looked around. Charlotte's Land Rover was in her spot. John knocked again. He wasn't going anywhere. Maybe he'd have to wait. He didn't care. He had to tell her what was in his heart. John knocked again and waited but he forgot to cover the peephole that time.

Charlotte was alone in her room. Her face was in a Chemistry textbook. She thought she'd heard the doorbell ring. It took a little while but she finally made it to the door. She looked out the peephole and could see a man in black. Then the features of his face gave him away.

"John." Charlotte stepped away from the door. She couldn't do it. *I told him I couldn't see him. Why is he here?* She paced around the apartment talking to herself out loud.

The doorbell rang again. John wasn't budging. Charlotte went back to the peephole to get another look. It was John all right. She was torn. She wanted to know why he was there. Why did he not do what she said? What would make him stand outside and wait?

It was starting to get really cold. John was starting to feel it in his bones. He thought about going home, getting his sleeping bag and coming back to camp out in front of her door. He knew sooner or later she'd come home or have to leave the apartment. John smiled a little and then knocked again.

"He'll just go away." Charlotte decided to be strong.

Then the doorbell rang again. Charlotte was startled. "He's not going away." She came to the moment of truth.

The door swung open as the light billowed out in the dark hall onto John. He took off his beanie and walked in.

"Is my hair all matted?" He pushed his hair down.

Charlotte smiled. "You look fine."

"I know what you said. I heard every word but I had to see you." John started to pace. He always paced when he was nervous.

"What are you doing?" Charlotte asked.

"I don't want to say anything wrong right now. I know you probably won't open that door the next time I'm outside in the cold, ringing, knocking, and ringing."

"John, you aren't making any sense," Charlotte said, hoping for a quick conversation.

The lock on the front door started to turn.

"Come back here with me," Charlotte called to John. He followed her into her bedroom. Charlotte shut the door. "It was probably Rachel but it's best if no one knows we're having a conversation."

John looked around. He was finally in her bedroom. A framed print of "The Kiss" by Gustav Klimt hung on the right wall. And a picture of Einstein sat over her desk and computer.

"I like your room," John said, smiling at her.

"Get on with it. Quit stalling."

"Okay. There's a lot I should tell you. You look really beautiful right now." Charlotte did something to John. It was hard for him to explain.

"I'm serious, John."

"Well, you have "The Glow" but there's so much more going on with you. I can feel it." John was trying to make sense of what he was saying.

"I shouldn't be talking to you. I'm engaged."

"I know, engaged to be married in two months. I'm not doing anything wrong." He looked up at her. "Look at your eyes, so gentle and alive. And your smile so happy, full, and peaceful." John put his hand on her face. Charlotte closed her eyes for a brief second.

"John, don't do this to me." Charlotte removed his hand. "You should go."

"I can't leave until you know something. I had a dream the other day with you. You were running to me."

"Do you know what would happen if Brian walked in right now?"

"Well, he's not here. I am," John said.

"John, this isn't fair."

"Will you just answer one question for me?" John asked.

"Then you'll leave?"

"Yes Charlotte. I promise I'll leave."

"Okay. One question."

"The night on the beach. I have to know. Did you feel something?" John stepped closer to Charlotte.

"Did I feel something?" Charlotte repeated, taking a step closer to him.

"Did you feel something?" John reached out his arms and pulled her to his chest.

"Is that all you want to know? Yes. Yes. I felt it. I remember the feeling like it was yesterday." Charlotte hugged John tight.

"I knew you did. And do you feel it right now?"

Charlotte smiled. "You only said one question."

John pulled away. "Do you feel it now?"

She nodded her head. Yes. She looked up at him. Her eyes twinkled as she moved her face closer to his. John didn't move.

Charlotte looked up into his eyes. John's lips were trembling. She smiled gently and pressed her lips into his lips. The kiss was electrifying, rockets launched, and tingles shot through each of their bodies. John pulled away first. Charlotte opened her eyes, looking at him. He couldn't say anything. Charlotte slowly backed away.

"What's wrong?" John asked.

"That shouldn't have happened. I'm engaged. I can't believe we actually . . . I'm a bad person." Charlotte was now letting the guilt control her emotions.

"You're not a bad person. And it's not your fault."

"You're right. It's not my fault. It's your fault. Why did you have to come over here?"

"Charlotte, look at me. I know you're confused but just focus on your feelings. How did it feel?"

She started to laugh. "How did it feel? How did it feel? Is that all you can say to me? I'm engaged. And I kissed you. I'm a cheater and I'm not even married yet."

"You're a great and amazing person. And you're not a cheater. The kiss happened. It simply happened," he said, trying to reassure her.

"Things don't just happen, John. There's a deeper meaning to everything we do."

"Is that the doorbell?" John heard it first. The doorbell rang again.

"Stay here. Actually, hide in the closet. And don't come out."

Charlotte looked in the bathroom mirror real quick. She stared at herself for a moment. *Am I happy?*

She rushed over to the front door. It was Brian. He entered and gave her a peck on the cheek. "Hey."

"Hi Brian." He walked in and poured himself a glass of water. "So, what are you doing here?" Charlotte asked nervously. She wanted him to leave immediately.

Brian sat down on the couch and turned on the TV. Charlotte picked up the remote and turned it off.

"You can't watch. Rachel has the VCR set to tape something."

He stood up. "Okay. Why don't we go to your bedroom?"

"You can't!" Charlotte grabbed his arm and led him to the door. "I want to turn in early. I'm exhausted. I'll see you tomorrow."

"But I just got here."

"I know. Thank you for that."

"Can we just cuddle?" Brian asked.

"No, Brian. We must be strong. We shouldn't even lie down next to each other."

Brian smiled. He kissed Charlotte's hand. "You're so right. It's getting late. I should go."

Charlotte kissed him on the lips. "Yes. It's so late. I have a big day at school tomorrow. Take care, hon."

She shut the door and locked it. Brian stood outside dumbfounded, especially when he heard the door lock.

Charlotte ran to her room. "John? John? You have to leave."

John came out from behind her clothes. "I don't want to leave."

"It's not your choice, John. It's mine." Charlotte was calling the shots.

He wanted to be stubborn and stay with her but something inside him said to comply with her wishes. He put on his coat, pulled down his beanie and headed for the door. Charlotte was right behind him.

"Are you sure?" John tried to press his luck.

"Open the door, John." Charlotte was not smiling.

He did as he was told and headed out into the cold. Snowflakes were falling slowly to the ground. He put out his tongue and caught a few with precision. John walked the same path back to his apartment. He knew without a doubt Charlotte had feelings for him. He wasn't sure, however, why she kicked him out. John surmised that she was confused as to what she needed to do. He could feel a little momentum shifting back his way. His only concern was that Charlotte would regret the kiss they had just shared.

Charlotte sat on her bed. She couldn't believe the feelings she had inside. For the first time she had a sentiment of doubt regarding Brian. Maybe it was the kiss. She knew it was more her fault than John's. Charlotte tried to rewind time with her thoughts. *I shouldn't have let him inside. And what was I thinking answering his questions. There was no reason to do that either. And I shouldn't have invited him into my bedroom. What was I thinking? Why did I let him kiss me? Wait. I kissed him.* She had kissed him.

She was torn between her feelings for John and her feelings for Brian. She had to talk to someone. Who could she talk to at eleven o'clock on a school night? There was only one person.

CHAPTER 26

John fell into bed and drifted off to sleep, peacefully thinking about Charlotte. He was more relaxed than he'd been since he arrived in Provo. He would have great, fantastic dreams that night about Charlotte and the life they'd have together. John smiled as his eyes faded and his head sunk into his pillow.

Charlotte pulled up to Y Mountain at about eleven-fifteen. It was snowing pretty hard outside and visibility was bad. She knocked lightly on the door. Hope opened it from the other side and let her in. Charlotte gave Hope a big hug.

They sat down at the kitchen table.

"Are you okay, Charlotte?" Hope could sense there was something wrong.

Charlotte didn't tell Hope anything over the phone. She just said she had to see her. Hope had heard that request before. She was the person people would turn to for advice. Hope never finished her psychology degree but she had a gift of talking to people and helping them see what they needed to do. For all intents and purposes she was a psychologist and Charlotte was one of her clients. The only difference was Hope was paid with cakes, brownies, a hug, or a simple "thank you." Hope didn't mind. She wanted to help people. Charlotte had sessions with Hope about twice a week. The great thing about Hope was her devotion to helping people. When Charlotte called she was fast asleep but she woke up just in time to pick up the phone. Hope had plenty of late night visits from distraught housewives, friends, and other clients, but Charlotte was a special client.

"Where do I start?" Charlotte let out a little laugh. She'd been crying.

"Why have you been crying?" Hope knew they needed to get right to it.

"Well, I'm engaged to Brian."

"Yes. I know that."

"And John, your brother has been around lately."

"Okay," Hope added.

"Well, earlier tonight I told John I couldn't see him anymore."

"Understandable. You're engaged," Hope said.

"So, he came over to my house anyway. And I let him in."

"You let John in." Hope knew where it was going.

"Yes. And then I didn't want to talk in the front room because someone might walk in on us. So, I took him to my bedroom."

Hope couldn't believe it. "Your bedroom?"

"My bedroom."

"What happened next?"

"John asked me a question."

"What question?"

"Basically he asked me if I still had feelings for him."

"What did you say?"

Charlotte shook her head. "I said yes. I couldn't lie."

Hope smiled. "No. You couldn't do that."

"Then John moved closer to me and I moved closer to him. And I kissed him. I feel so bad. I'm a cheater."

"You kissed him? Don't you mean he kissed you?"

"No. I kissed him but he kissed me back."

"I understand, Charlotte but John made the first move, right?"

"No. I pulled him in and kissed him," Charlotte admitted.

Nate walked into the kitchen quietly and opened the fridge. It startled Charlotte. "Who's that?" she asked.

Hope was used to it. "Don't worry about him. It's only Nate. He snacks late at night."

Charlotte laughed. "Every night?"

"Every single night. Sometimes I wake up and he's gone. Then I come in the kitchen and he's making a sandwich," Hope said.

"That's weird."

"Enough about Nate. Charlotte, you've got a problem on your hands. What happened next?"

"The guilt hit me hard after we kissed. I told John to leave and then I called you. What should I do?"

Hope put her hand on Charlotte's shoulder. "You know the way I work. I would never say this is what you have to do."

"Then what advice can you give me?"

"I think the best thing I could say is to follow your heart."

"Follow my heart."

"Yes," said Hope.

"That sounds so simple."

"Charlotte, some of the best choices we make in life are sometimes the easiest."

"What if your heart is torn?" quizzed Charlotte.

Hope smiled again as her eyes twinkled with wisdom. "I've found through experience that your heart can't be torn between two different things or in your case, people. It's your brain telling your heart that. Listen and then follow your heart."

"Hope, I think you're right. Thank you." Charlotte grabbed Hope and hugged her. "I don't know how but you seem to always say the right thing."

"Charlotte, don't forget. Listen, follow, and you'll know," Hope reiterated.

"I understand." Charlotte stood up. "I'm sorry for coming by so late." She gave Hope another hug.

"Don't worry Charlotte. I'm always here. Just remember what I said."

Charlotte put her hand over her heart. "I will."

John was still dreaming. His face was innocent like a child. He was standing on the beach looking out into the ocean. Then she came. She surfaced out of the water, gliding toward him in a bright white dress. Charlotte stepped onto the beach and then in a full sprint ran at John tackling him to the ground. She sat on his chest, pinning his arms beside him.

"Mercy. Say mercy, John." Charlotte waited for him to give in.

"Never. Never." He laughed, enjoying the moment.

Then he heard a ring, a ringing noise. He looked around the beach and couldn't understand where it was coming from. The ringing intensified and John put his hands over his ears. It was no use. John sat up in his bed and the dream faded away.

His cell phone was the culprit. It wouldn't stop ringing. He looked at the caller ID. It was Hope. She left a "911" message.

"Great." He tossed off the covers and picked up the phone.

"Hey. What's up? It's two o'clock in the morning. And I was having this great dream." John yawned a couple of times.

"John Michael Edwards, I don't care. Get over here, now."

"All right. I'll be there in five. What if you fall asleep waiting for me?"

Hope was defiant. "If you don't get over here this second, John, you're going to get it."

John didn't want to be on Hope's bad side. He often referred to it as the "dark side."

"I'm leaving right now."

He threw on his coat over his pajamas, put on a beanie and his Birkenstocks. Hope meant business.

CHAPTER 27

John sat in front of Hope. He'd seen that look before. He wasn't sure exactly what she'd say first. She just glared at him.

"What were you thinking, John?"

He smiled. "What do you mean?"

"And don't smile. You think it's funny don't you?"

"What are you talking about Hope?"

"Charlotte. Charlotte left here an hour ago. She told me everything."

"Everything? This is between her and me. Why do you always have to stick your nose in my business?"

"First off, it's not your business and second she's a client."

"A client? Are you nuts? You can't have clients if you're not a licensed psychologist."

"Why? Because I never finished my degree. Do you want Luke to go to a day-care center all day and never see me? I couldn't do that. Don't try and change the subject, John. We're talking about Charlotte." Hope was a little upset. She'd always wanted to go back to finish her schooling and deep down she knew she'd maybe never get the chance again.

"I'm sorry, Hope. I didn't mean it that way."

Hope wiped away a tear. "It's funny John but you've always been able to say just the right things to hurt me."

John put his hand on her shoulder to console her. "I really am sorry. You're a wonderful mother. That was your priority. I didn't mean it, okay?"

"I just hope you understand that it's not easy starting a marriage with a honeymoon baby," she said.

"Would you do it any differently?"

Hope smiled. "Not a chance."

"So, you want to know about Charlotte?" John asked.

"No. I want to know what's going on in your head."

"I didn't tell you before because I was afraid I'd lost her." John laughed. "But it's way beyond that now. Hope, I love her. I really think I do."

"You think? That's not how it works. You have to know, John."

"Fine. I know I love her."

Hope stood up, poured herself a glass of water. "Want anything?"

"No. Look at me Hope. I'm serious. I'm a lovesick fool. I don't want to lose her forever."

"Does she know everything? Have you told her everything?"

It was the last thing John wanted to think about. And he knew it was coming. He should've told Charlotte the truth when he was in her bedroom. He had planned to tell her everything but when the time came he couldn't do it. He was afraid she'd never want to see him again. He couldn't risk that.

Hope repeated herself. "Did you tell her?"

"No." John tried to fight the guilt. He'd won a couple of rounds during the time he was in Provo but in other rounds he had pummeled and was left defenseless. Guilt was funny like that. And a lie was like cancer. John's lie was eating a hole in his heart. His whole reason for being with Charlotte was a lie. A LIE! John knew no matter what happened down the road the truth would surface and it would crush Charlotte. That was the last thing he wanted. Deep down in his soul he just wanted her to be happy.

"John? John?" Hope brought him out of the trance of thoughts.

"Yeah."

"When are you going to tell her the truth?"

John's face tightened. "Is it better to hurt someone by telling them the truth or just let them find out down the road . . .?"

Hope cut him off. "You don't have to finish that. You should never avoid the truth."

John knew she was right. Why did she always have to be right? He realized his whole ploy to win Charlotte was a fraud. The whole foundation of his plan was based on a lie.

"Hope, I shouldn't have lied to her." He knew what he had to do. "Do you think she'll forgive me?"

"I don't know John."

John put his face in his hands. He sat there for a long time, a thousand life times it seemed.

Hope started to rub his back. "You're a good person, John. You just made one bad mistake."

"I know." His response was quiet like a whisper.

"You can never have something beautiful and precious if it starts out ugly. Soon the ugliness and lies will consume all of the beauty."

John stood up. "I have to face the music."

Hope gave him a big hug. "I love you, John. I don't see another choice."

He thought of those last words as he drove home from Hope's: "I don't see another choice." It was true and honest. John wished he'd been true and honest from the beginning.

CHAPTER 28

John stayed up the rest of the night. Actually by the time he came home from Hope's, it was already five am. He sat there quietly thinking about Charlotte. He knew she was usually out the door by nine. He forced himself to put on his shoes and his jacket. He knew he'd have to make the lonely walk down to her house. He went outside and began the descent. He tried to turn back more than a dozen times. He'd made up his mind. She had to know the truth.

It was a warm day for December. Charlotte was eating breakfast: a banana and wheat toast with raspberry jam. No one else was up in her apartment. They never were. Charlotte liked to get an early start. She read her scriptures and then would hit the textbooks. She was disciplined and focused. She sat down in the living room and picked up her textbook. She held her highlighter, ready to go to work. She read a sentence and then found herself reading it again and again. It was no use. She couldn't concentrate. She had to tell Brian what happened with John and how she felt when they kissed. Charlotte knew it would eat her up inside until she told him the truth.

Someone knocked on the door. Charlotte got up quickly and looked out the peephole. It was John.

"Please, open up." He wanted to forget why he was there.

Charlotte tried to fight it. Then her cell phone rang. She picked it up.

"Charlotte, it's me. I'm outside. I need to tell you something."

"John, it's not a good time."

"What I have to say will clear everything up. Please let me in." John pleaded.

Charlotte looked out at John. Then she could hear the static. John mouthed the word "Please!"

She opened the door and John stepped inside. He shut the door and stood right next to the wall. Charlotte sat down on the couch. "Do you want to sit down?"

"No. I'll just stand. I . . . I don't know how to tell you." John was fighting the urge to lie to her again.

"What do you want to tell me?"

"You look really beautiful today."

"Thank you." Charlotte blushed.

"That's not it. You do look beautiful but it's something else. I've done something and I have to tell you."

"Okay."

"I knew. I knew you were engaged when I met you the first time at that restaurant. Your parents saw me at a friend's wedding and told me. And then after that Hope told me. I definitely knew you were engaged. I definitely knew," John said and looked away from Charlotte.

"What?" Charlotte asked, surprised.

"I know it's horrible. I lied to you."

"To my face."

"I know. It was tearing me up inside. And I don't have a computer job in Salt Lake. I was following you all along."

Charlotte stood up. She couldn't take it sitting down. "And the time you ran into me on campus."

"It was totally set up. I knew your schedule, when you left class, everything. And I timed it perfectly."

"Everything?" Charlotte had no smile to give. "You deceived me."

"I didn't want to do it. When I heard you were engaged

something in me clicked. And I remembered you. I remembered us."

"Remembered us? There wasn't ever an us. We kissed once until last night. Was that part of your plan, too, for me to kiss you?"

"Charlotte, I care about you. And the kiss meant a lot to me." He tried to express his feelings. It was a bad attempt.

"I can't believe this, John. I thought you were different. And I was wrong," Charlotte exclaimed.

John's palms were sweating as he ran his hands through his hair. "I know. I'm so ashamed of myself. I'm so pathetic. I never thought I'd do anything as desperate as lie to you and that's why I know I don't deserve you. I don't know how you can ever forgive me. And I don't blame you," John said. He looked up and smiled at her. Charlotte looked away. "But you have to understand. I do love you. And I think there will always be a piece of you in my heart forever. And I hope you're always happy with Brian."

"John—" Charlotte tried to get a word in edge wise.

"I hope you're always happy." John opened the door. "Don't worry, you'll never see me again. I'm leaving Provo tonight. Have a happy life. I'm totally unworthy of you. I'm such a loser. And I'm sorry. I'm so very sorry. And I don't think I'll ever be more sorry in my entire life." He walked out the door.

John did it. He finally told the truth. He thought he'd feel good right away but he didn't; he felt empty and lost. He walked alone to his apartment. John knew it would take a long time to get over Charlotte. He wasn't sure if he'd ever be able to forget. There was nothing he could do. He knew he truly didn't deserve to be with her. It was that simple. And by her response neither did she. He replayed in his head the look on her face when he said he lied to her. It was like the world came crashing down on top him. The look she gave him.

John wanted to be out of Provo as soon as possible. It was a mistake to even come to Provo at all. He started to load things into his car: the guitar, the laptop, snowboard (never used it), and armfuls of clothes. His exodus was not a planned endeavor and the car was being packed without regard to any order. He didn't care. He didn't have time for order. It hurt him to know he couldn't have Charlotte, but it was even more punishing to know she lived three buildings down.

There was a knock at John's door. Maybe it was Charlotte. Maybe she could forgive him. He sprinted to the door and opened it. It wasn't her.

"What's up, Will?"

"John, buddy. Good to see you." Will was laying it on extra thick.

"I'm out of here, Will. Heading back to L.A. I should never have left L.A." John went back to his room to pack. Will followed.

"No man. You don't want to do that."

"And why is that, Will? The only girl I think I have ever truly loved doesn't want anything to do with me. And she lives here. I can't live here." John continued pulling clothes out of the closet.

"You're leaving because of a girl. Do you know how many times I've been engaged?"

"I don't care." John wanted Will to say his peace and leave him alone.

"Four times in the last six years. Do you know why?" John wasn't paying attention. Will walked over to a pile of clothes and hung them back up in the closet. "Because there's always a smarter, more beautiful, funnier girl around the corner. This is the Mormon Mecca, man. Don't give up because one girl broke your heart."

John laughed. "So, that's why you're not married. Well, I'm

personally never going to be able to find another girl like Charlotte around the corner. She was different."

"Stay bro. I'll set you up with whomever you want. Give me measurements. Or maybe a girl that looks like Heidi Klum or Laetitia Casta. You tell me. They're everywhere."

"That's great," John said.

"So, you're staying?" Will quizzed.

"I can't have what I want. And now I have to live with that and move on. Well, I'm moving on." John picked up a load of clothes and headed outside to his car.

"John, are you crazy? You shouldn't leave. Just date a different girl every night. You never have to see that Charlotte chick ever again."

John closed the trunk. "That's the problem, Will. If I'm near her, I'll want to see her."

"Then see her again. Who cares?"

"Will, have you ever been in an argument you knew you were going to lose no matter what?"

"Of course," Will said.

"You're losing." John shook Will's hand. "Thanks for the job. Have a good time up here."

"You're making a mistake, man." Will patted John on the back.

"By the way, Will. The pat on the back thing kind of creeps me out. Be good."

John's car was a mess but it was packed and ready to go. He put his key in the ignition, backed up and left The Belmont for the final time. He slipped Al Green into his CD player. John sang along to "I'm Still In Love With You" as he turned onto the I-15 South. He waved goodbye to Provo and goodbye to Charlotte.

Charlotte was sitting in her class. She was fidgeting.

Something was bothering her and it wasn't the drool on Dr. Walker's face. She excused herself to go to the bathroom and took her backpack. She wasn't going to come back. John really hurt her to the core when he revealed his lies to her. Charlotte drove in silence. She wondered why John could hurt her so much. Did she love him? Would there always be a piece of him in her? She sped toward The Belmont and pulled up in front of John's place.

She knocked on the door. His roommate answered it.

"Is John here?" Charlotte wanted inside.

"No. He's gone." The roommate responded.

"Gone? Can I see his room?"

"Go ahead."

Charlotte walked back to the empty room. It was bare like no one had lived there at all. The floors were recently vacuumed and some wire hangers were in the closet. John was gone, like a ghost. She sat down on the naked bed and took a deep breath.

"Maybe it is for the best." She stood up and walked outside. She wondered where he was and if he was thinking about her.

She had one last resort. She drove up to Y Mountain for answers. It was like déjà vu, only it was light outside.

"Hope. I need to talk to you."

Charlotte walked past all of the day-care toddlers watching Barney.

"You okay?" Hope could see she was troubled.

Charlotte's face was flushed. "He's gone. John's gone."

"I thought that would happen." Hope smiled lightly.

"Why did he leave like that?"

"John is actually a simple guy. He knew what he did to you was wrong and then he realized he didn't deserve someone like you. He did tell you everything?"

"Yes. He said he already knew I was engaged. And he lied to me about some other things, too."

"How do you feel Charlotte?"

"I hate him. I mean I don't like what he did. And now it seems like my choice is easier."

"There you go. Listen to your heart. So, when are you guys getting married again?" Hope asked.

"In two months," Charlotte whispered.

Hope smiled. "If you feel like you did the right thing, then you did the right thing."

"Do you think John will be okay?" Charlotte wondered.

"I think John will be fine."

Charlotte stood up. "Thank you again. This is becoming an every day thing now." She gave Hope a hug.

"Charlotte, listen to your heart and follow it."

"I know." Charlotte was on her way to the front door.

"Charlotte?"

"Yeah." She stopped.

Hope walked over to her. "Did John tell you he quit his job, basically threw his life away, packed up his car, and moved up here only for you?"

Charlotte was caught by surprise. "No. He didn't."

"He probably should have told you that too." Hope smiled. "Have a good day."

Charlotte walked to her car. She was going to meet Brian at noon for lunch. They had a lot to talk about. Charlotte knew Brian would understand. She wouldn't be able to eat a thing but Brian had to know everything—everything that happened.

John's drive home to L.A. was quite possibly the loneliest and most solitary trip any man had ever made. He listened to every depressing and lovesick CD in his case. He had to get it all out of his system.

When he stopped at Wendy's in St. George, he started to cry uncontrollably. He looked down at each French fry and cried like a baby. Every patron at in Wendy's looked at him. It was like clockwork, every time he picked up a fry and dipped it into the ketchup, he'd sob like a little child.

The closer John got to the California border, the better it was. He was listening to Chris Isaak's *Forever Blue* album. It was perfect for heartbreak. He thought maybe that's what he would do. He'd write an album for Charlotte to get her out of his head. John had heard of one of his friends writing a mysterious screenplay to get over an ex-girlfriend. He would write an album with lovesick, solemn, and depressing songs all about Charlotte. First, he needed to learn how to play the guitar. He was already starting his new life. He'd dedicate many hours a day to learn how to play the guitar. And then he'd write a bunch of songs and make his album. That was "The Plan." John thought about that phrase, "The Plan." He wasn't sure he liked it anymore. He decided he would erase it from his vocabulary. Never again. He'd use synonyms, anything. John would never ever ever say "The Plan" again.

Charlotte sat across from Brian. They were already deep into their talk. The talk was about everything.

"Brian. I'm sorry for not seeing what was going on."

"No problem honey. Aren't you hungry?"

Charlotte looked right at him. "So, John is gone. And he was in love with me but he lied to me."

"Of course he lied to you." Brian re-emphasized her point.

"Right. So, John's no longer in the picture," Charlotte sighed.

Brian reached across the table and grabbed her hands. "I'm glad you chose me. I'm the happiest man alive."

Charlotte smiled. She knew she had to tell him everything. She was listening to her heart and finally following it. Her heart was erupting inside her as she squeezed Brian's hands.

CHAPTER 29

John got back to California just in time for the annual Edwards Christmas dinner at his parents house in Huntington Beach. He knew everyone would be there. Hope, Nate, and Luke were flying down and the rest of his siblings, their spouses and children would also be present.

He sat at the dinner table surrounded by his entire family. He smiled but was in pain. It wasn't like a headache either. His heart was on fire and he couldn't put out the flame. It would take time, a lot of time.

Brittany, John's three-year-old niece noticed he wasn't eating. "Uncle John, my mommy says you should eat your vege-bles. Corn is good. Yum." Brittany took her fork to her corn. Everyone at the table laughed. John gave his best fake laugh and then pretended to eat. Hope looked over at him. She knew he wasn't himself.

John picked up his plate and took it into the kitchen. He started to wash all of the left over food into the garbage disposal. His mother, Linda, stood behind him. "Are you okay John?"

"I'm fine, Mom. Just a little tired. I'm going to take a nap."

John headed up the stairs. He went into his old room. There were pictures of surfers and waves, a map of Europe, and a framed print of "The Kiss" by Gustav Klimt. He dropped back onto the bed. He wanted to sleep for days. He didn't need food, company or entertainment, only the bed.

The whole family gathered into the game room and then the fun began. The karaoke machine was revved and ready to go. One of John's older brothers named Dan was nicknamed by the family as the "Karaoke King." He traveled to Japan for business and saw first hand where karaoke came from. Dan could sing any song. He picked up the microphone and began with "Wanted Dead Or Alive" by Bon Jovi. The karaoke session during the holidays at the Edwards' home wasn't for the weakhearted. Everyone in the family could sing and perform. And everyone tried to top each other. Stephen and Linda sat back and watched with joyous smiles. It was so good to have their whole family together. Next it was Stephen's turn. The song, his favorite, was "Old Time Rock N' Roll" by Bob Seger. Stephen was probably the most animated of them all. He never followed the beat of the song and used a raspy, almost talking method of singing. It was classic Stephen. Everyone else in the room was rolling with laughter.

John tried to go to sleep. There was no way. The karaoke would go on forever deep into the night. Hope opened the door to his room slowly with Luke in tow.

"Are we disturbing you?"

"No. Come in." John sat up. Who was he kidding? It was Christmas. "I know I need to quit feeling sorry for myself."

"What?" Hope questioned.

"You don't have to say anything," John said.

"No. I'm next downstairs. And I'm singing Summer Lovin' and I need a John Travolta. Will you sing it with me?"

John laughed. "We're next?"

John and Hope held mics in their hands and focused on the screen.

"Summer lovin' had me a blast." He had a great voice. Then Hope was Olivia. "Summer Lovin' happened so fast." They continued going back and forth as the rest of the Edwards family watched from the sidelines. John and Hope were natural together. That song had a special past for them. They finished and then the applause came.

Linda grabbed John and kissed him. "You have such a good voice, John."

"Yeah. We could be rich with that voice," Stephen said, putting in his two cents.

Everybody laughed and then the next karaoke song began. They all sat around for hours singing Harry Chapin's "Cat's In The Cradle", Joe Cocker's "Up Where We Belong", and Pat Benatar's "Hit Me With Your Best Shot", and all the girls sang The Bangles' "Manic Monday."

John was laughing again. Now he was laughing for real. His family was the greatest. He knew most people said that about their families but he didn't know where he'd be without his family. It was the greatest support group anyone could possibly have.

Dan was addicted to karaoke. His wife thought it was a disorder. He and karaoke couldn't stop. He stood up, grabbed the mic and went into Journey's "Don't Stop Believin.'"

"Just a small town girl livin' in a lonely world. She took the midnight train going anywhere." Dan was a ringer for Steve Perry. The rest of the family joined in on the chorus. "Don't stop believin', Don't stop believin.'"

The karaoke continued till the break of dawn and the last person standing was Dan. They were all karaoke'd out. John looked around at his family. They were the coolest. He knew they'd always be there for him no matter what, even if he went to prison. Not that starting a life of crime was part of John's New Year's resolutions. It was just a ridiculous example of their unconditional love toward him.

CHAPTER 30

Christmas came and went. John had great memories and heart to heart talks with his brothers and sisters. He would never be alone. Hope and her family flew back to Provo and John went up to his apartment in L.A. He looked at the calendar, December 31st, New Year's Eve. "Great."

John was invited to a huge New Year's Eve dance in Long Beach at the Pyramid at Long Beach State campus. He didn't want to go but he knew he'd end up there anyway. He needed to get back in the field, even though he was scared of the ball.

He had a lot to do when January 1st came rolling around. He thought first he would crawl on his hands and knees to his old boss and beg for his "monkey labor" job back. Then he'd get a new hobby, maybe start surfing again. He thought about writing resolutions but he never followed through. He hoped that the New Year would be different. He would just let things happen. No expectations! He would just live and life would just happen. John Lennon said, "Life is what happens to you when you're busy making other plans." John's New Year resolutions or goals included being a better person, being honest, caring, giving, and to be selfless. He knew things could've turned out differently with Charlotte if he had been more that kind of a guy. John had a smile on his face. He knew he'd been a little intense over the years. He wanted everything NOW! Now, he realized that's not the way it works. His goals needed to be more realistic.

John thought about Charlotte everyday. He knew she'd be in his thoughts for the rest of his life. Time had passed and he realized what he had done was for the best. He threw on some Diesel jeans and a black turtleneck. He had to move on and the dance in Long Beach was the perfect place to start. He put on his shoes and headed out the door. Then he came back in and picked up his cell phone. He never left the house without his cell phone.

He drove down Sunset Blvd. toward the 405. His cell phone rang. He looked at the caller ID. Nothing came up. He thought maybe it was a wrong number. The cell phone rang again.

"Hello?" John finally picked it up.

"Shut up. And don't say a word. Go to the one special place for us."

"Charlotte?" John tried to hide his excitement. She wasn't gone.

John wasn't going to the dance at the Pyramid after all. His new strategy of letting life come to him was already paying dividends.

He cruised at about 90 mph all the way to Corona Del Mar and toward the cove where they both kissed for the first time.

It was nine-thirty when he made it down to the sand. He looked around. Nobody. John sat down on the sand. He'd wait. He was positive it was Charlotte who called him. And the cove was the special place. He knew that for sure. Well, not for sure. Maybe there was somewhere else. No, John was certain it was the cove. He looked around to make sure he was in the right cove. He retraced his steps in his head. John decided it was the right place and he'd just wait because he knew she'd come. He'd wait all night and the next day for her.

John looked at his watch. It was 11:45 p.m. on New Year's Eve. He must've imagined her voice or something. He shook his head: Who was he fooling? There was no way he'd be able to forget her. He was hopeless. He thought he'd heard her voice, and next he thought he'd imagine seeing her. He stood up and shook off the sand. He was all alone on the beach on New Year's Eve. How pathetic! John was never going to find anyone. He'd be alone forever. He was a single, lonely, pathetic fool. The uncle who never got married and liked to read fantasy books and went to movies by himself. John was going to be the guy everybody would talk about, "What happened to him? I thought he had so much potential."

He looked up into the sky and laughed. He thought he should be committed. John would never be the same. He knew Charlotte was like oxygen and he needed her to breathe, to feel, and to live. John watched the waves crashing onto the shore. He wanted to run and jump in the ocean and swim away and never turn back. Instead John turned his back to the ocean and started to walk back up the beach toward his car.

"Where are you going?"

John recognized the voice. It was Charlotte's voice.

"Am I imagining you again?" He called out to the darkness.

Charlotte walked out of the shadows and stood next to him. "I've been watching you. Why are you leaving?"

"I don't know." John couldn't believe it was her, flesh and bones, Charlotte.

"Why did you leave Provo?"

"I didn't want to complicate things for you."

"Who gave you the right to decide what was best for me?" Charlotte had an intense tone in her voice.

"Nobody. But aren't you getting married to Brian?"

Charlotte stepped closer to John. "Quiet. I'm not done with you. I have more questions. What did you feel when we kissed here so long ago?"

John smiled. "I felt peace. And I felt like I found someone I'd known forever."

"And that's why you left me?"

John was still in shock. "I didn't feel worthy to be with you."

"Worthy? Isn't that my choice? To decide whether or not I want to be with you."

"I guess it is. What are you doing here?" John asked.

"I choose you, John. I choose you."

John's entire body was filled with emotion. He wanted to laugh and cry all at the same time. "What?"

"I choose you." Charlotte moved even closer. Her smile was blinding and serene.

"I don't understand."

"I was always in love with you. Since the first time I saw you. I just knew. But you didn't see it. It took a long time and I waited. When I couldn't take it any longer I started to date guys like Brian. Guys completely the opposite of you. I thought it would help me to move on." Charlotte looked into John's eyes. "And it was working until you called me out of the blue. I was going to marry Brian."

John laughed. "In two months."

"Right. In two months. You see, John . . . you were my dream. I always dreamed of being with you. I just never thought it could ever happen. So I waited. I waited a long time. And I couldn't wait any longer."

"Well, I'm here." He smiled and grabbed her hands.

"And that's why I made you wait here at the beach. I knew if you couldn't wait for a couple of hours then you didn't deserve me."

John smiled. "And I passed the test."

"Barely. What, do you have ADD or something?" Charlotte said, laughing.

"No. I thought your voice was in my head. I thought I was chasing a dream."

Charlotte laughed. "Well, guess what. I'm real." She meant every word. Tender emotion swelled inside her.

John looked up at Charlotte. He tried to hold back the

tears. Charlotte was already gushing. "Can we start over? I'm John." He kissed her hand.

"I'm Charlotte."

John wiped away her tears and smiled. "What's next year going to be like?"

Charlotte looked at John's watch. "How much time do we have left on this one?"

They held hands and counted down together. "Ten, nine, eight, seven, six, five, four, three, two, one. Happy New Year!"

Charlotte pulled John into her. "Kiss me already."

John accepted the challenge and their lips met. It was an explosion of time, passion, and most importantly, love. The sky behind them was a roaring kaleidoscope of red, white, green, blue, and every color under the sun in the form of fireworks bursting over the ocean. John and Charlotte didn't see any of the fireworks in the sky. They were too busy making their own. And their hearts were one. They had no plan, just each other. Sometimes that's enough.

ABOUT THE AUTHOR

David Steenhoek is twenty-eight, single, and lives in Huntington Beach, California. He graduated from Brigham Young University with a Bachelor's Degree in Political Science and received a Master's Degree in Education. He taught autistic children in South Central Los Angeles for two years. He also worked for two years at the Mosaic Media Group film company in Beverly Hills. Currently he attends the American Film Institute in Hollywood. This is his first novel.